Cold Comfort

Michael Ferguson

Published by Michael Ferguson, 2024.

COLD COMFORT

First edition. September 13, 2024.

Copyright © 2024 Michael Ferguson.

ISBN: 979-8227922366

Written by Michael Ferguson.

Table of Contents

Chapter 1: Disgraced

D r. Henry Talbot woke to the familiar stench of stale alcohol and unwashed sheets, his head pounding as if a jackhammer were going off inside his skull. The blinds in his dingy Manhattan apartment were drawn, barely letting in any light. It suited him. Darkness was a comfort now, shielding him from the harsh realities of his fallen existence.

He groaned, rolling over and fumbling for the half-empty bottle of whiskey by the bed. His hand knocked over a pile of crumpled papers—old case notes, therapy records, and newspaper clippings, all yellowed and worn from his constant revisiting. The remnants of a life that once held promise. He took a long swig from the bottle, wincing as the liquor burned down his throat, momentarily dulling the ache that lived inside him. But no amount of alcohol could drown out the memories.

They say when you hit rock bottom, there's nowhere to go but up. Henry knew better. He'd been falling for a long time now, past the bottom, into a dark abyss of regret, self-loathing, and addiction. Once, he'd been someone. Once, they'd called him a genius, a pioneer in the field of psychotherapy. His name had been spoken with admiration at professional conferences. Henry Talbot, the man with all the answers, the therapist who could crack the toughest cases. He had helped so many people unlock the mysteries of their minds, guiding them through the maze of their traumas and fears.

And yet, when it came to his own mind, Henry was as lost as anyone else.

His career had imploded two years ago, when the scandal broke. He had crossed the line with a patient—a young woman named Emily Harper. It was all over the media for weeks: "Top Therapist Accused of Ethical Breach," "Dr. Talbot's Fall from Grace," "Emily Harper Still Missing, Foul Play Suspected."

It had started innocently enough, he told himself. Emily had come to him broken, battered by life and by the man who controlled her every move. Simon Harper, her husband, was a well-respected psychiatrist himself, a colleague of Henry's in fact. They'd crossed paths at a few conferences, even shared a drink or two. But Emily's sessions were different. She had been desperate, scared, convinced Simon was going to kill her if she didn't escape. She had cried in his office, telling him her darkest fears, pleading for his help.

And Henry had crossed the line. Somewhere along the way, his professional detachment had eroded. He had cared too much. Wanted too badly to save her. Emily had become more than just a patient; she had become an obsession. He had lost his objectivity, let his emotions get tangled in the mess of her life, and then—God help him—he had crossed that final, unforgivable boundary.

He had slept with her.

That was the end of everything. When Emily disappeared a few months later, Simon had gone straight to the media, accusing Henry of seducing his wife, of manipulating her fragile state of mind. The ensuing scandal destroyed Henry's career. The state board had stripped him of his license, and the court of public opinion had shredded what remained of his reputation.

The worst part? Henry didn't even know if Emily was alive. She had vanished without a trace, leaving behind a storm of questions and suspicions. Simon had blamed him, of course, insinuating that Henry had something to do with her disappearance. But Henry knew that wasn't true. Or at least, he thought he knew. His memories of that time were so hazy, so muddled by the drugs and alcohol he had turned to in the aftermath.

Now, two years later, Henry had become a ghost of his former self. The man in the mirror was gaunt, with sunken eyes and a scruffy beard. His once-steady hands trembled as he reached for another cigarette from the pack on his nightstand, lighting it with shaky fingers. He inhaled deeply, the smoke filling his lungs, temporarily numbing the gnawing emptiness inside him.

A loud bang on the door jolted him from his thoughts. He flinched, cursing under his breath as he stubbed out the cigarette in a half-empty coffee mug. Another knock, more insistent this time.

"Talbot!" The voice from the other side was sharp, impatient. "Open up! It's your landlord."

Henry groaned, dragging himself out of bed. His joints ached as he shuffled toward the door, pulling it open just enough to peer through the crack. Mr. Sykes, the greasy-haired landlord, stood on the other side, arms crossed and a scowl on his face.

"You're late again on the rent," Sykes said, his eyes narrowing. "I've been more than patient with you, but this is the third month in a row, Talbot. You either pay up by the end of the week, or you're out. Got it?"

Henry nodded, barely registering the words. He mumbled something that sounded like agreement and slammed the door shut, leaning his back against it as he sank to the floor. He could barely muster the energy to care anymore. Eviction? Fine. Let it all burn.

But then, as he sat there in the quiet of his crumbling apartment, something caught his eye. A slip of paper had been shoved under the door. His name was scrawled on the front in black ink. Frowning, Henry reached for it, unfolding the note with trembling fingers.

She's still alive.

His heart skipped a beat. He read the words again, his mind struggling to process them. Emily. It had to be about Emily. Who else could it be?

Adrenaline shot through him, cutting through the fog of his hangover. He staggered to his feet, the note clutched tightly in his hand as he rushed to his desk. Papers flew everywhere as he rummaged through old files, looking for anything—any clue—that could explain this.

Two years. Two long, agonizing years of silence, of not knowing. And now, out of nowhere, this cryptic note. Was it a cruel joke? A sick prank? Or was it real?

Henry's hands shook as he pulled out Emily's case file, the one he had kept despite everything. He had read it a thousand times before, memorized every detail, but now, with the note in his hand, it all felt new again. He scanned the notes, looking for something—anything—that could help him make sense of it all.

Emily Harper. Age 28. Former patient. Reported missing on October 3, 2022. Last seen leaving her husband's office after an argument. No trace of her had been found since.

He flipped through the pages, his eyes skimming over the details of their sessions. She had been terrified of Simon, convinced he was controlling her, watching her every move. She had spoken of escape, of disappearing completely. But she had also spoken of fear—fear that Simon would find her, fear that he would never let her go.

And now, this note. She's still alive.

Henry's mind raced. If Emily was alive, where had she been all this time? And why had she stayed hidden? He needed answers. He needed to know the truth.

He grabbed his coat from the back of the chair, shoving the note into his pocket as he headed for the door. His heart pounded in his chest, a mix of hope and dread swirling inside him. He didn't know what he would find, but he couldn't ignore this. Not now. Not after all this time.

As he stepped out into the cold, gray streets of Manhattan, a thought crossed his mind—a whisper of doubt that chilled him to the core.

What if Emily didn't want to be found?

The streets were as unforgiving as they always had been. Henry shuffled through the crowds, his eyes scanning every face, every corner, as if expecting Emily to materialize before him. His mind was racing, but the alcohol still clung to his thoughts like a heavy fog. He needed clarity, but the temptation to drown himself in another drink was always there, nagging at the back of his mind.

He made his way to the bar where he used to meet with old colleagues before everything fell apart. The place had lost its luster now, but it was familiar. Comforting in its own way.

The bartender gave him a nod of recognition, pouring him a whiskey without asking. Henry downed it in one gulp, the burn helping to focus his thoughts, if only for a moment. He pulled out the note, staring at it as if it might reveal more if he just looked hard enough.

She's still alive.

The words taunted him, a puzzle with no clear answer.

"Another?" the bartender asked.

Henry shook his head, tucking the note back into his pocket. He needed to stay sharp. He needed to think. But the booze had been his only companion for so long, it was hard to imagine making it through the night without it.

As he left the bar, a sense of purpose began to take hold. He didn't know who had sent the note, but he was going to find out. He was going to find Emily, one way or another.

The streets were quieter now, the sun setting behind the skyline as darkness crept in. Henry pulled his coat tighter around him, his breath visible in the cold air.

Henry sat at his cluttered desk, the dim light of a single lamp casting long shadows over the scattered papers and empty bottles. The smell of stale whiskey and cigarettes lingered in the air. His hands trembled as he picked up the small slip of paper that had arrived in the mail earlier that day. It was a simple note, typed in an untraceable font, with no return address.

"Emily Harper is alive."

The words echoed in his mind, over and over again, like a refrain he couldn't shake. For two years, he had been haunted by Emily's disappearance. The case had consumed him—destroyed his career, ruined his relationships, and pushed him further into the spiral of addiction. And now, out of nowhere, this note had reignited the fire of his obsession.

"Alive," he whispered to himself, the weight of the word pressing down on him.

He leaned back in his chair, exhaling a deep, ragged breath. His gaze fell on the stack of old case files that littered his desk. Emily's file was there, of course, sitting at the top, its pages dog-eared and yellowing with age. He reached for it, flipping it open to the first page, where her name was scrawled in his once-neat handwriting: Emily Harper, age 28. Trauma and anxiety.

Her face flashed in his mind—dark, haunted eyes that always seemed to carry the weight of the world. Emily had been different from his other patients. She hadn't just been troubled—she had been desperate. Desperate to escape a life of fear and control. Desperate to be free of Simon, her manipulative and powerful husband. And Henry had been the one she had come to for help.

But instead of helping her, he had ruined everything. His inappropriate involvement had been a violation of the sacred trust between therapist and patient, and it had cost him everything. After Emily disappeared, the authorities had scrutinized every detail of their relationship. His license was revoked. His reputation obliterated.

And now this note. A promise that perhaps, somewhere, she still existed.

He closed the file and stood, moving toward the small window of his apartment. Outside, the city was alive, pulsing with energy, but Henry felt utterly detached from it. His life had become a prison of isolation and regret.

With a sudden burst of resolve, he turned back to the desk and began rifling through the papers. There had to be something in her case notes, something he had missed—some clue that could lead him to her. He hadn't allowed himself to touch these files in over a year, but the note had sparked something deep inside him.

As he sifted through old therapy notes, his mind drifted back to their last session. He could still hear her voice in his head, soft but determined.

"Henry, I can't keep living like this. He's watching me all the time. I need to disappear. You're the only one who can help me."

Her plea had been raw, and he had felt powerless against it. He had crossed lines he knew he shouldn't, but he had convinced himself it was to protect her. It had all unraveled so quickly.

A sharp pain stabbed through his skull, forcing him to pause. The headaches were getting worse. He stumbled toward the kitchen and opened the cabinet, pulling out a small orange bottle. Popping a couple of amphetamines into his mouth, he washed them down with a gulp of whiskey.

He returned to the desk, eyes scanning the notes more quickly now. Page after page of therapy sessions—her fears, her anxiety, her desire for freedom. But then he came across a note from their final session, a line that stood out like a neon sign in his fogged mind.

"Everything is going to change soon, Henry. You'll see."

At the time, he had taken it as part of her usual cryptic nature, a woman trapped in a web of her own mental turmoil. But now, in the light of this new message, it seemed more deliberate. Like she had known something he hadn't.

His eyes darted back to the note he had received, sitting on the corner of the desk. Was this her way of reaching out to him now, after all this time? Was this some kind of game, or was she truly alive?

The questions flooded his mind, and the only way to get answers was to start searching.

He grabbed his coat and stumbled out of his apartment, ignoring the dizziness in his head. His first stop would be the office—his old office. He hadn't been there since his license was revoked, but it was where all the files were kept. It was where Emily's case began, and it was the only place he knew to start.

The building hadn't changed much since he'd last been there. A few lights still glowed in the windows, but the halls were empty. His old office was untouched, save for the thick layer of dust that coated the surfaces. The memories hit him like a wave—sessions with patients, the calm voice of his secretary, the quiet buzz of therapy in progress.

He moved to the filing cabinet in the corner, hands shaking as he pulled open the drawer marked H through J. There it was. Harper, Emily. He pulled the file and dropped it onto the desk. As he thumbed through the documents, he found the final sessions recorded in his notes. The tension between Emily and Simon had been unbearable. Simon's control over her had reached a fever pitch.

A small photograph fell out of the folder, landing face-up on the desk. It was a picture of Emily, her expression tense, her eyes wide with fear. The image was dated just days before her disappearance.

He stared at the picture, trying to recall every detail of those final days. Simon had come to his office, too. He'd demanded to know what was going on between Emily and him. That confrontation had been the beginning of the end.

Suddenly, something caught his eye. At the bottom of one of the therapy notes, written hastily in the margins, was a single word: "Wednesday."

Henry frowned. There was no context, no explanation—just "Wednesday." What did it mean?

His mind raced. Was it a day she had planned something? Was it a day connected to her disappearance? The note hadn't mentioned a specific date, but "Wednesday" felt significant now.

He took a deep breath and scribbled the word into his notebook, determined to follow this new lead. But as he closed the file, the weight of his situation settled over him once more. Two years of silence, of guilt, of drowning in his own failures—and now he was chasing after ghosts.

He needed help, but who could he trust? Simon? No, Simon was the last person who would give him any answers. In fact, Simon was probably part of the problem. Henry had no doubt the man had something to do with Emily's disappearance. But proving it—finding out the truth—was going to take more than just rifling through old notes.

There was one place that might hold some answers, though. The rehabilitation center where Emily had checked in for anxiety treatment. The same place that had failed her, just as he had.

He left the office, pulling his coat tighter around him as he stepped out into the cold night air. The clinic was only a few miles away, but it felt like another world. A place where broken people went to be fixed—or to disappear.

The clinic was in worse shape than he remembered. The walls were cracked, the paint peeling in long, jagged strips. The front desk was abandoned, and the lights flickered weakly overhead. Henry felt a shiver run down his spine as he made his way inside, the musty smell of neglect hanging in the air.

He approached the receptionist's desk, but there was no one in sight. A bell sat on the counter, but it looked as though it hadn't been used in years. He tapped it hesitantly, the faint ring echoing down the empty hallway.

After a few moments, a woman emerged from a back office. She was older, her face worn with lines of stress and exhaustion.

"Can I help you?" she asked, her voice raspy and tired.

Henry cleared his throat, trying to pull himself together. "I'm looking for information on a former patient. Emily Harper."

The woman's eyes flickered with recognition, but she quickly masked it with a blank expression. "We don't give out patient information. It's confidential."

"I was her therapist," Henry said, leaning forward slightly. "She disappeared two years ago. I'm just trying to find out what happened to her."

The woman hesitated, glancing down the hallway before lowering her voice. "Emily Harper... she wasn't the only one who disappeared from here. A lot of people... they check in, and then they're just gone."

Henry's heart skipped a beat. "What do you mean?"

"Look, I don't know much. But people talk. And Emily... she was scared. Real scared. I think she was planning to run."

"Run? Where?"

The woman shook her head. "I don't know. But she talked about someone... someone who was helping her. She never said who, but I think she had a plan."

Henry's mind raced. Emily had been planning something all along—something bigger than he had realized. But who had been helping her? And why had she vanished without a trace?

"Do you have any records? Anything that might show who she was in contact with?" he asked.

The woman glanced nervously down the hallway again before nodding. "I might have something. Wait here."

She disappeared into the back room, leaving Henry alone with his thoughts. His heart pounded in his chest as he tried to piece everything together. Emily had been scared, but she hadn't been helpless. She had been planning her escape all along—and someone had been helping her.

When the woman returned, she handed him a small folder. "This is all we have on her. But be careful. If she's still alive, there's a reason she's staying hidden."

Henry took the folder, his hands trembling as he opened it. Inside, he found a single page of notes, along with a list of names and phone numbers. None of the names were familiar to him, but one number stood out: it was scribbled in the margins, next to the word "Wednesday."

He stared at the number for a long moment before closing the folder. Whoever this was—whoever had been helping Emily—it was time to find out the truth.

Back at his apartment, Henry sat down at his desk and dialed the number. His pulse quickened with each ring, his mind racing with possibilities.

After a few moments, a voice answered.

"Hello?" The voice was deep, unfamiliar.

Henry hesitated for a moment before speaking. "I'm looking for information about Emily Harper."

There was a long pause on the other end of the line, followed by a quiet chuckle.

"Emily Harper is dead."

Henry's blood ran cold.

Chapter 2: Ghosts of the Past

Henry Talbot sat at his desk, staring at the old recorder in front of him, his finger hovering over the play button. The machine was outdated, one of the relics of his previous life—his old office, the clinical white walls, and the certificates that used to line them all gone now. The recorder was one of the few pieces he had taken with him when everything else fell apart.

It was heavy in his hand, just like the memories it contained. Emily Harper. He hadn't listened to these tapes in nearly two years. Her voice, her fear, her desperation—all of it was imprinted in his mind, even after all this time. But now, with the note sitting on his desk, claiming she was still alive, the weight of those memories felt unbearable.

He pressed play, and the static-filled recording crackled to life. Then came her voice, shaky but determined.

"I don't know how much longer I can stay. Simon... he's always watching, Henry. Always. I don't think I'll make it out alive if I stay with him."

Henry closed his eyes, remembering that session. It had been one of the last. She had been so scared, trembling as she sat across from him, her hands clutching a tissue so tightly it tore in half.

He remembered the intensity in her eyes, the haunted look that had consumed her as she spoke about her husband. Simon Harper was no ordinary man. He was wealthy, powerful, and well-connected. A man who knew how to get what he wanted.

A man Henry had once worked with, long before Emily became his patient.

He paused the tape and stared at the small recorder. Why had he let it get so personal? He'd crossed every line of professional ethics, but he hadn't cared. He told himself it was because Emily needed help, and Simon was a monster. But was that the real reason? Or was it something more twisted? A desperate attempt to feel needed, to save someone—anyone—so he could ignore the wreckage of his own life.

Henry clicked the tape back on, listening to more of her last words.

"I've been thinking about leaving for a while, but it's hard. He has people everywhere. He knows every move I make. Even here—I'm not sure he doesn't know I'm talking to you."

That had been the moment, Henry realized, when everything had shifted. He hadn't known then just how deep Emily's fear went. He had assumed, like many therapists do, that it was part of her anxiety, her trauma. But what if it had been real? What if Simon really had been watching, controlling everything?

He replayed the last sentence over and over again in his head. Even here—I'm not sure he doesn't know I'm talking to you.

Had Simon known? Had he been watching them all along?

His stomach turned as he realized just how far out of his depth he had been. Emily hadn't just been a patient. She had been something more, a complicated puzzle that he hadn't been able to solve. And in the end, she had disappeared, leaving nothing behind but questions. And now, two years later, the questions were still haunting him.

He lit a cigarette, staring at the recorder as if it could give him answers. It couldn't. It was just a machine, after all. And Emily was just a voice on a tape—one he couldn't seem to forget.

"I need you to help me, Henry. Please. If I stay, he'll kill me."

He remembered how her voice had cracked, her eyes brimming with tears. She had always looked at him like that, pleading, desperate. And he had wanted to save her. But saving her had meant losing everything.

He took a long drag on his cigarette, the smoke curling up toward the ceiling. Emily's last sessions had been the breaking point for him. He had become too involved, too invested. It had started as a simple case—an abused woman needing help to escape. But it had turned into something much darker, something Henry hadn't been prepared for. His career, his reputation, his life—they had all unraveled because of her.

He wondered now, as he sat in his dingy apartment, surrounded by the remnants of his past, if it had all been worth it. Emily had vanished without a trace, and he had been left to pick up the pieces of his shattered life. But had he ever really known her? Or had she been manipulating him from the start, using him as a pawn in her own twisted game?

The more he thought about it, the more he realized how little he actually knew. Emily had come to him with her story of abuse, her pleas for help. But had it all been true? Or had she been playing him, just like she had played Simon?

He flicked the cigarette into the ashtray and stood up, pacing the room. The walls felt like they were closing in on him, the weight of his obsession pressing down on his chest. He couldn't shake the feeling that he had missed something, that there was more to Emily's story than he had ever realized.

The note on his desk seemed to mock him, its message simple but devastating: Emily Harper is alive.

Could it be true? Or was it just another lie, another piece of the puzzle meant to drive him further into madness?

He grabbed the tape recorder and threw it across the room. It hit the wall with a dull thud, the tape popping out and unraveling onto the floor. But even as the machine lay broken, the memories continued to swirl in his mind.

Emily's last sessions had been a blur of fear and desperation, her words twisting into a narrative that had consumed him. She had talked about escaping, about leaving Simon and starting a new life. But she had never been clear on how she planned to do it.

"I'm thinking about disappearing," she had said in one of their final meetings. "Just... vanishing. Starting over somewhere else. It's the only way I'll ever be free."

And then, a few days later, she had done exactly that. Vanished. No one had seen or heard from her since.

Henry had spent months searching for her, following every lead, every clue. But they had all led to dead ends. Eventually, he had given up, resigned to the fact that she was gone. But now, with the note in hand, everything had changed.

He sat back down at his desk, the weight of the past two years pressing down on him. The memories of Emily's last sessions played out in his mind like a broken record, her voice haunting him, reminding him of his failure.

He pulled out a notebook from the drawer and flipped through its pages. It was filled with notes, thoughts, and scribbles—his attempt to make sense of it all. But none of it added up. Emily had been terrified of Simon, convinced he was going to kill her. But had he? Or had she simply used that fear as a cover for her own escape?

As he stared at the pages, a sudden thought struck him. What if Emily hadn't been running from Simon at all? What if she had been running from something—or someone—else?

Henry's mind raced as he considered the possibility. Had there been someone else in Emily's life, someone she hadn't told him about? The idea seemed ridiculous at first, but the more he thought about it, the more it made sense.

Emily had always been vague about her past, her relationships. She had told him about Simon, about the abuse, but she had never gone into detail. What if there had been another man, someone she had been trying to escape from all along?

Henry stood up again, the energy surging through him. He needed answers, and the only way to get them was to find Emily. He had to know the truth—whether she was alive, whether she had been playing him all along.

He grabbed his coat and headed for the door. The apartment felt stifling, the walls too close, the memories too heavy. He needed to clear his head, to think. The city outside was his only escape.

As he stepped out onto the street, the cold air hit him like a slap in the face, waking him from his daze. He walked aimlessly for a while, the note crumpled in his hand, his mind spinning with possibilities.

If Emily was still alive, he had to find her. He had to know what had really happened. But where would he even start?

The note had been vague, offering no real clues. But it had been enough to reignite his obsession, to pull him back into the darkness he had tried so hard to escape.

As he wandered through the city, his thoughts drifted back to their last session. There had been something in her eyes that day, something he couldn't quite place. Fear, yes. But also something else. Determination? Resignation? He couldn't be sure.

He stopped in front of a bar, the neon lights flickering in the window. His hand trembled as he reached for the door, the temptation almost too much to resist. He could go in, have a drink, forget about everything for a while. But he knew it wouldn't last. The memories would come back, stronger than before.

With a sigh, he turned away from the bar and continued walking, his mind still racing. He didn't know where he was going, but he knew he couldn't stop now. Not until he had the answers he was looking for.

Emily was out there, somewhere. And Henry was going to find her, no matter what it took.

Henry stood outside the brownstone, its once pristine exterior now weathered and worn, mirroring his own decline. It was the last known address of Emily Harper, a place he hadn't visited since their final therapy session. The memory of that day flooded his mind—the way she had sat in the chair across from him, her eyes hollow, her voice trembling with fear and uncertainty. She had seemed desperate then, clinging to him for help, for salvation. But now, after everything that had happened, Henry wasn't so sure that was the full story.

The street was quieter than he remembered, the autumn leaves swirling around his feet as he approached the front door. The landlord had been reluctant to give him any information over the phone, but Henry's persistence—and a small bribe—had eventually secured him an appointment to look around. He wasn't sure what he expected to find, but the anonymous note had reignited something within him, a desperate hope that maybe, just maybe, Emily was still out there.

He rang the doorbell and waited, glancing around nervously. The neighborhood wasn't what it used to be, much like himself—once prosperous, now teetering on the edge of decay. He could see a few people moving about on the street, but no one seemed to pay him any attention.

Finally, the door creaked open. A balding man with a gruff demeanor stood in the doorway, peering at Henry with suspicion. "You're Talbot?" he asked, his voice rough from years of cigarette smoke.

"That's right," Henry said, trying to muster some semblance of authority. "I'm here about the apartment."

The man grunted and stepped aside, letting Henry into the dimly lit foyer. The walls were covered in faded wallpaper, and the smell of mildew lingered in the air. Henry followed the landlord down a narrow hallway, his footsteps echoing off the creaky wooden floors.

"Place has been empty for a while," the landlord said over his shoulder. "After the girl disappeared, no one wanted to rent it. Can't blame 'em. People get spooked by that kind of thing."

Henry nodded absently, his mind racing with thoughts of Emily. He hadn't been able to shake the feeling that her disappearance was more than just a simple case of a woman running from an abusive husband. There were too many unanswered questions, too many loose ends.

They stopped in front of a door near the end of the hallway. The landlord fumbled with a ring of keys before unlocking it and pushing the door open. "Go ahead," he said, stepping back to let Henry enter first.

The apartment was small and sparsely furnished. A worn-out couch sat against one wall, and a small kitchen area was tucked into the corner. Dust covered the surfaces, and the air felt thick with neglect. Henry's eyes scanned the room, taking in every detail, looking for anything that might give him a clue about Emily's whereabouts.

"She didn't leave much behind," the landlord said, leaning against the doorframe. "Cops came through, took whatever they thought was important. But if you want to look around, be my guest."

Henry nodded and stepped further into the room. He moved slowly, methodically, as if retracing Emily's steps. He couldn't help but feel a strange sense of familiarity, as though her presence still lingered in the air. It was unnerving, but he pushed the feeling aside and focused on the task at hand.

He walked over to the small desk near the window, his fingers tracing the outline of a notebook that had been left behind. The pages were blank, but the spine was creased as if it had been used before. He flipped through it, finding nothing of significance. Frustrated, he tossed it aside and turned his attention to the bookshelf.

Most of the books were standard fare—novels, self-help guides, a few psychology textbooks. But one title caught his eye: The Art of Disappearing. It was a thin, paperback book, the kind you might find at an airport bookstore. Henry pulled it off the shelf and opened it, his eyes scanning the introduction. It was a guide to starting a new life, complete with chapters on how to sever ties with your past and create a new identity.

He felt a chill run down his spine. Had Emily been planning this all along? The thought was unsettling, but it made sense in a way. She had been desperate to escape Simon, and with his connections and resources, simply running away wouldn't have been enough. She would have needed to disappear completely.

Henry flipped through the book, searching for any markings or notes Emily might have left, but there was nothing. He tossed it aside and continued searching the apartment, growing more frustrated by the minute. There had to be something here, some clue that would lead him to her.

His eyes drifted to the closet. It was slightly ajar, as if someone had opened it in a hurry and forgotten to close it properly. Henry walked over and pulled the door open, revealing a row of empty hangers and a few boxes stacked on the floor. He crouched down and opened one of the boxes, hoping to find something useful.

The first box contained old clothes—nothing remarkable. But the second box was different. It was filled with papers—old bills, letters, and receipts. Henry sifted through them, his heart racing as he searched for anything that might give him a lead.

At the bottom of the box, he found a stack of photographs. Most of them were of Emily—some taken at parties, others in more intimate settings. But one photo stood out. It was a picture of Emily standing outside a building, her arm around another woman. Henry recognized the building immediately—it was the rehabilitation center where Emily had sought treatment for her anxiety and addiction.

Henry's pulse quickened. The woman standing next to Emily looked familiar, though he couldn't place her right away. He studied the photo, trying to remember where he had seen her before. Then it hit him—she was one of his former patients, a woman named Mia who had also sought treatment at the rehab center.

Mia had always been quiet during their sessions, rarely speaking about her personal life. But now, seeing her in this photo with Emily, Henry realized that there had been more to her story than she had let on.

He stood up, clutching the photo in his hand. This was it—the connection he had been looking for. Mia had to know something about Emily's disappearance. And if she had been at the rehab center with Emily, there was a chance that she might still be there.

Henry turned to the landlord, who had been watching him from the doorway. "I'm done here," he said, slipping the photo into his pocket. "Thanks for your help."

The landlord grunted and stepped aside as Henry walked past him and out into the hallway. As he made his way back to the street, his mind raced with possibilities. Mia was the key to unlocking this mystery—he was sure of it.

But as he stepped outside and felt the cool autumn air on his face, a sense of dread settled over him. He was treading dangerous ground. The rehab center was notorious for its shady dealings, and if Simon Harper had any connection to it, getting involved could be a death sentence.

Still, Henry knew he couldn't back down now. He had come too far. Emily was out there somewhere, and he had to find her—no matter the cost.

As he made his way to the rehab center, his mind drifted back to the last time he had seen Emily. She had been vulnerable then, fragile, and in need of help. But now, Henry wasn't so sure. The more he uncovered, the more he realized that he had never really known her at all.

The rehab center loomed in the distance, its cold, sterile facade a stark contrast to the warmth and vibrancy of the city around it. Henry felt a knot form in his stomach as he approached the entrance. He had been here before, but this time was different. This time, he wasn't just a therapist checking in on a patient—he was a man on a mission, desperate for answers.

The receptionist barely looked up as he entered, her eyes glued to the computer screen in front of her. "Can I help you?" she asked, her voice flat and disinterested.

"I'm here to see Mia," Henry said, trying to keep his voice steady.

The receptionist glanced up, her eyes narrowing as she studied him. "Do you have an appointment?"

"No," Henry admitted. "But it's important."

The receptionist sighed and tapped a few keys on her keyboard. "She's not here," she said after a moment. "Hasn't been for a while."

Henry felt a pang of disappointment. "Do you know where she went?"

The receptionist shook her head. "Sorry. I'm not at liberty to discuss patient details."

Henry clenched his fists, frustration boiling inside him. He had come so close, only to hit another dead end. But he wasn't about to give up. There had to be another way to find Mia, to get the answers he needed.

As he turned to leave, a voice called out from behind him. "Hey, you looking for Mia?"

Henry spun around to see a man leaning against the wall, his arms crossed over his chest. He was thin, with sunken cheeks and dark circles under his eyes—a typical addict, by the looks of him.

"Yeah," Henry said, stepping closer. "Do you know where she is?"

The man smirked and nodded. "Maybe. But it'll cost you."

Henry reached into his pocket and pulled out a crumpled bill, handing it to the man without hesitation.

"She's staying at a halfway house on the east side," the man said, pocketing the money. "Not too far from here."

Henry felt a surge of relief. Finally, a solid lead. "Thanks," he said, turning to leave.

But as he stepped out into the street, a sense of unease settled over him. He was getting closer to the truth, but the more he uncovered, the more dangerous the situation became.

Chapter 3: The Rehab Connection

The dilapidated sign hanging crookedly from the rusted brackets read "Harrison Wellness Center," its faded letters barely legible through the grime. Henry Talbot squinted up at it, his head pounding from the cocktail of amphetamines and bourbon he'd indulged in the night before. The clinic stood in stark contrast to the posh establishments of his past life, a monument to his own fall from grace. The building itself was an ugly block of crumbling concrete, overrun with graffiti and grime. It was a far cry from the pristine, well-appointed offices he once frequented.

He hesitated at the entrance, his mind churning with a mix of anxiety and anticipation. Emily Harper had been a patient here, and the place held secrets he needed to uncover. With a deep breath, he pushed open the heavy, wooden door. It creaked ominously, the sound echoing through the empty lobby.

The interior was as grim as the exterior. The walls were stained and peeling, and the floors were covered in a layer of dust that had settled over the years. Henry approached the reception desk, where a woman sat behind a glass partition, her face obscured by a haze of cigarette smoke. She looked up with an expression of practiced indifference.

"Can I help you?" Her voice was tired, as if she had been answering this same question for decades without much enthusiasm.

"I'm looking for some information about a former patient, Emily Harper. She was here a while ago," Henry said, trying to sound authoritative.

The woman's eyes narrowed slightly. "That name doesn't ring a bell. This place has seen more comings and goings than I can keep track of."

Henry glanced around the lobby, noting the worn chairs and scattered magazines that had seen better days. "Could I speak with someone who might remember her? Perhaps someone from the counseling staff or the administrative side?"

The receptionist's expression softened just a touch. "You might want to talk to Doris in the back office. She's been here a long time. But I'm not sure how much she'll remember. The turnover here is pretty high."

Henry nodded, a feeling of unease settling in his stomach. The fact that the receptionist seemed unsure about Emily's presence here only added to his growing sense of dread. He followed the woman's directions and made his way to the back office.

Doris was a gray-haired woman with tired eyes and a no-nonsense demeanor. She looked up from her desk as Henry entered, her gaze assessing him with a mix of curiosity and suspicion.

"Yes? What can I do for you?" she asked.

"I'm Henry Talbot. I'm looking into a case related to a former patient, Emily Harper. I understand she was treated here."

Doris's expression remained neutral, but there was a flicker of recognition in her eyes. "Emily Harper, you say? It's been a while since she was here. What do you want to know?"

"I'm trying to find out what happened to her after she left this clinic. Anything you can share might help."

Doris leaned back in her chair, considering him. "I remember Emily. She was... troubled, to say the least. She had a lot of issues, but she was also a bit of a mystery. Not everyone who comes through these doors is memorable, but she stood out."

Henry's heart skipped a beat. "Why was that?"

Doris's gaze grew distant. "She had a certain intensity about her. She was always on edge, always looking over her shoulder. And there were rumors about her being involved in something... darker, though I couldn't tell you specifics."

"Rumors? What kind of rumors?"

"Nothing concrete. You know how it is—people talk. Some said she was involved with people who weren't exactly clean. Others thought she was just paranoid. Either way, she left abruptly, and no one seemed to know where she went."

Henry's frustration grew. "Did she leave any clues or personal items behind? Anything that might give me a lead?"

Doris shook her head. "I don't recall anything specific. But if you're looking into this, you might want to talk to some of the former patients. They might have more to say. Some of them are still around, though many have moved on or disappeared themselves."

Henry nodded, feeling a mix of hope and apprehension. He was about to leave when Doris's voice stopped him. "One more thing. Be careful. This place has its share of secrets, and not everyone who comes here is exactly trustworthy."

Henry thanked her and left the office, his mind racing with possibilities. The mention of rumors and the warning from

Doris only heightened his suspicion. As he walked through the clinic's dingy corridors, he spotted a few individuals lingering in the waiting area, their expressions hollow and distant.

He approached a man sitting alone in a corner, who looked up at him with weary eyes. "Hey, do you have a minute?"

The man hesitated, then nodded. "Sure, what's up?"

"I'm looking for information about a former patient, Emily Harper. Did you know her or hear anything about her?"

The man's face grew guarded. "Emily Harper? Yeah, I remember her. She was... different. Always seemed like she was on edge."

"Do you know what happened to her after she left here?" Henry pressed.

The man shifted uncomfortably. "I heard she got involved with some bad people. It was a bit of a buzz among the patients. But I don't know much more than that. I've moved on from this place and try not to look back."

Henry's frustration mounted. "If you know anything, please—anything at all could help."

The man looked around nervously before leaning closer. "Look, I heard she was trying to get away from something, someone. And she was looking for help, but she was scared. People like her—they don't just vanish without a reason. There's something more to it."

Henry took in the man's words, his mind racing with possibilities. "Thank you. Anything you remember could be important."

The man nodded, visibly relieved to be done with the conversation. Henry left the clinic feeling more determined than ever. The hints of darkness and the sense of secrecy surrounding Emily's case were becoming clearer, but they also deepened the mystery.

As he walked back to his apartment, Henry's thoughts churned. The shadows at the clinic were more than just physical—they represented the deeper, more sinister layers of the case he was trying to unravel. Emily Harper had been entangled in something dangerous, and as he continued his search, he realized that uncovering the truth might be more perilous than he had anticipated.

Henry Talbot's footsteps echoed through the deserted hallways of the dilapidated clinic, each step weighted by the sense of dread and anticipation that had come to define his days. The air inside was stale, heavy with the smell of old coffee and disinfectant, a mix that did little to mask the underlying stench of decay. The once-promising institution now lay in a state of disrepair, its walls lined with peeling paint and its floors marred by long-forgotten stains. The clinic was a relic of better days, a testament to broken dreams and failed promises.

He had returned to the clinic's reception area, where the fading remnants of a once-thriving facility now gathered dust. The receptionist's desk, long abandoned, stood like a ghost of its former self. Henry's eyes fell on the nameplate that still lingered there, tarnished and covered in grime: "Margaret Collins, Office Manager." A sense of recognition struck him—Margaret Collins had been a name from his past, an old acquaintance in the field who had once worked closely with him. He recalled her as a diligent worker, someone who had been part of the inner circle of the mental health community.

The room was now empty, save for a few broken chairs and a desk cluttered with outdated paperwork. Henry's mind raced as he remembered the whispered conversations he had overheard about Margaret. The words "corruption" and "hidden agendas" came back to him, whispered with a hint of fear. Was Margaret Collins involved in something more sinister than he had ever imagined?

His investigation had already unearthed several troubling connections between the clinic and Simon Harper. Simon's influence had spread far and wide, leaving a trail of corruption in its wake. But now, Henry needed concrete evidence to connect the dots between Simon's financial dealings and the clinic's dark underbelly. Margaret Collins, he hoped, could provide the key.

Henry took out his phone and dialed a number he had found in his notes—a contact he had identified as someone who might still have connections with the clinic. The line rang for what felt like an eternity before a raspy voice answered.

"Hello?"

"Is this Margaret Collins?" Henry asked, trying to keep his tone steady despite the adrenaline surging through him.

"Yes, who's asking?" Margaret replied, her voice tinged with curiosity and suspicion.

"This is Dr. Henry Talbot. I used to work in the mental health field, and I'm looking into some old connections. I believe you might be able to help me."

There was a moment of silence on the other end of the line, and Henry could almost picture Margaret's furrowed brow as she processed the information. Finally, she spoke.

"I see. Well, I suppose I owe you some answers. What is it that you're looking for?"

Henry took a deep breath, gathering his thoughts. "I'm investigating a case involving Emily Harper. She was a patient at this clinic a while back. I need to know more about her time here and if there's any link between her disappearance and the clinic's financial activities."

Margaret's response was slow and cautious. "Emily Harper, you say? That's a name I haven't heard in a while. Her case was... peculiar. I'm afraid I don't have much information on her personally, but I can tell you that things weren't as straightforward as they seemed."

Henry's heart raced. "Can we meet? I need to speak with you in person."

There was a brief pause, and then Margaret replied, "Alright. Meet me at the café on 4th and Main in an hour. It's safer that way."

The call ended, leaving Henry with a mix of anticipation and apprehension. He made his way out of the clinic, the old building's oppressive atmosphere still clinging to him. As he walked to the café, he reviewed the information he had gathered so far, mentally preparing for the meeting with Margaret Collins.

The café was a small, unassuming place nestled between a bookstore and a florist. Its cozy interior offered a stark contrast to the grim atmosphere of the clinic. Henry arrived early, choosing a secluded corner table where he could observe the entrance and remain discreet. He ordered a black coffee and waited.

Margaret Collins arrived precisely on time. She was a middle-aged woman with a stern demeanor, her appearance marked by a no-nonsense attitude. Her dark hair was pulled back into a tight bun, and she wore a tailored suit that hinted at her former role in the professional world. She scanned the café before spotting Henry and making her way over.

"Dr. Talbot?" she said, her voice firm as she approached the table.

"Yes, Ms. Collins," Henry replied, standing to greet her. "Thank you for meeting with me."

Margaret took a seat and ordered a coffee before settling in. "What's this about Emily Harper? Why are you so interested in her now?"

Henry leaned forward, his eyes locked on Margaret's. "Emily's disappearance has haunted me for a long time. I'm trying to piece together what really happened. I believe there's a connection between her case and some shady dealings at this clinic."

Margaret's expression grew wary. "You're not the first to dig into that case. There were always whispers about corruption and cover-ups, but I don't know what you hope to uncover now."

Henry took out his notes and placed them on the table. "I have reason to believe that Emily's disappearance wasn't just a random event. Simon Harper, her abusive husband, has financial ties to the clinic. I'm trying to understand the full extent of this connection."

Margaret's eyes widened slightly, but she maintained her composure. "Simon Harper? That name carries a lot of weight. He was involved in some high-profile cases. If he's tied to this clinic, then we're talking about something serious."

Henry nodded. "Exactly. I need to know more about the clinic's financial records and any connections to Simon's enterprises. Can you help me access this information?"

Margaret sighed, taking a sip of her coffee. "Accessing financial records isn't something I can just hand over. The clinic has become a hub for various shady dealings, and digging too deep can be dangerous. But I might be able to point you in the right direction."

Henry leaned in, his voice low. "I'm willing to take the risk. I need to find out the truth, no matter the cost."

Margaret studied Henry for a moment, her gaze piercing. "Alright. There was a financial officer named Steven Gray who managed the clinic's accounts. If there's anything hidden, he would have known about it. However, he disappeared a while ago, and there's no record of his departure. Finding him might be your best bet."

Henry's mind raced as he absorbed this new lead. "Do you have any idea where I might find Steven Gray?"

Margaret hesitated before responding. "I don't have a direct lead on his whereabouts, but he was known to frequent a bar called The Raven's Nest. It's a dive bar on the outskirts of town. If he's still around, that might be where he's hiding."

Henry made a note of the bar's name, feeling a surge of hope. "Thank you, Margaret. This information is invaluable."

Margaret stood up, preparing to leave. "Be careful, Dr. Talbot. There are dangerous people involved in this mess. You're treading on thin ice."

Henry nodded, watching as Margaret left the café. He finished his coffee and left the café, determined to follow the new lead. The Raven's Nest was his next destination, and he hoped it would bring him closer to unraveling the truth about Emily's disappearance.

As he made his way to the bar, the weight of his investigation felt heavier than ever. The pieces of the puzzle were beginning to fall into place, but the full picture remained elusive. Henry knew that finding Steven Gray and uncovering the clinic's secrets would be crucial to solving the mystery. But with each step, he was also aware of the danger that lurked in the shadows, threatening to consume him if he wasn't careful.

The Raven's Nest was a far cry from the upscale bars Henry once frequented. It was a dimly lit establishment with a worn-out atmosphere, its neon sign flickering intermittently. The air inside was thick with the smell of cigarette smoke and stale beer. Henry entered cautiously, scanning the room for any signs of Steven Gray.

The bar was sparsely populated, with a few patrons nursing their drinks at the bar and scattered tables. Henry approached the bartender, a grizzled man with a weathered face and a wary expression.

"Evening," Henry said, trying to sound casual. "I'm looking for someone who used to come around here. His name is Steven Gray."

The bartender's eyes narrowed. "Steven Gray? Haven't heard that name in a while. He used to come in here a lot, but he disappeared some time ago. Haven't seen him around in months."

Henry's heart sank, but he pressed on. "Do you have any idea where he might have gone? Anything at all would help."

The bartender shrugged. "Sorry, can't help you much. He was always a bit of a loner, didn't talk much about his personal life. But if you're looking for information, you might try asking around. Some of the regulars might know more."

Henry nodded, taking the bartender's advice. He made his way around the bar, striking up conversations with the few patrons who were willing to talk. Most of them were tight-lipped, their faces revealing little. But as the night wore on, he managed to glean a few snippets of information that suggested Steven Gray had left town abruptly.

Frustration gnawed at Henry, but he was determined to follow every lead. He left The Raven's Nest with a renewed sense of urgency, knowing that finding Steven Gray was essential to unraveling the clinic's secrets and uncovering the truth about Emily Harper.

As he drove back to his apartment, the city lights blurred by his fatigue, Henry's thoughts were a chaotic whirlwind of connections and possibilities. The investigation was leading him into deeper and darker territory, but he knew that the answers he sought were within reach. The name Steven Gray had opened a new avenue of inquiry, and Henry was resolved to follow it wherever it led.

The road ahead was fraught with danger and uncertainty, but Henry's resolve was unshaken. The pursuit of the truth had become his obsession, and he was willing to risk everything to uncover the reality behind Emily's disappearance.

Chapter 4: Lost in the Fog

Henry Talbot stumbled through the narrow, dimly lit corridor of his apartment building, clutching the worn edges of his coat to stave off the biting cold. His footsteps echoed hollowly against the concrete walls, and the oppressive silence only amplified the disquiet he felt inside. He fumbled for his keys, his hands trembling uncontrollably, and nearly dropped them twice before finally managing to unlock his apartment door.

Once inside, the warmth of the small, cluttered space enveloped him like a shroud. The apartment was a chaotic mess of discarded bottles, crumpled newspapers, and empty prescription pill bottles scattered across the floor. The once-grand furniture was now shabby and covered in dust, a reflection of Henry's own state of disrepair. He dropped his coat on a threadbare armchair and staggered toward the kitchen, where a half-empty bottle of whiskey awaited him.

The whiskey burned his throat, a temporary reprieve from the unrelenting turmoil in his mind. He had been drowning his sorrows in alcohol and amphetamines for months, but recently, the effects had begun to worsen. The blurred lines between reality and hallucination had become more pronounced, and Henry was caught in an ever-tightening spiral of paranoia and self-delusion.

As he sank into his recliner, the dim glow of the streetlamp outside cast eerie shadows across the room. His thoughts were a chaotic jumble of fragmented memories and distorted perceptions. The more he tried to focus on Emily Harper's case, the more elusive the details became. Her face, once so clear in his memory, now appeared as a vague, shifting silhouette.

The previous day's events had left him agitated. His visit to the clinic had only deepened his sense of confusion. The former patients he had spoken to had been evasive, their words shrouded in half-truths and innuendo. They hinted at something dark and insidious within the clinic, but none were willing to elaborate. Their silence had only fueled Henry's paranoia, making him question what he had missed, what he had failed to see.

He closed his eyes, trying to block out the disorienting swirl of images in his mind. His memories of Emily's therapy sessions had begun to bleed into his hallucinations, creating a nightmarish landscape where past and present intertwined in disturbing ways. He recalled her pleading eyes, her trembling voice as she spoke of her abusive husband, Simon Harper. Yet, the more he dwelled on these memories, the more they seemed to twist and warp, morphing into something unrecognizable.

The whiskey bottle, now nearly empty, was abandoned on the floor as Henry's vision began to blur. The room around him seemed to pulse with a strange, rhythmic vibration, and the shadows on the walls appeared to shift and writhe like living entities. He gripped the armrests of his chair, trying to steady himself, but the effort only made his head spin faster.

In his disoriented state, Henry's mind drifted back to the moments of clarity he had experienced during his brief encounters with the clinic's former patients. They had spoken in hushed tones, their faces etched with fear and uncertainty. One name kept surfacing in their fragmented stories: Steven Gray. It was as if the name was a key to unlocking a deeper layer of the mystery, a thread that might unravel the whole tangled web.

Henry's thoughts were interrupted by a sudden, sharp pain in his chest. He gasped for breath, his heart pounding erratically. The combination of his deteriorating mental state and the physical toll of his addiction had left him on the brink. He tried to calm himself, taking slow, deliberate breaths, but the anxiety only seemed to escalate.

The oppressive silence of the apartment was broken by the distant, rhythmic thud of a heartbeat. It was a sound that seemed to emanate from within his own body, yet it resonated with an eerie familiarity. Henry's head lolled back against the chair as he struggled to make sense of the disjointed sensations engulfing him.

In the midst of his confusion, a vision of Emily Harper materialized in his mind. She appeared as she had during their last session, her eyes filled with a mixture of desperation and determination. Her voice, distorted by the haze of his mind, echoed in his ears, pleading for help, for understanding. But as he reached out to grasp her hand, the image dissolved into a swirling vortex of shadow and light.

Henry's breathing became more labored as the hallucinations intensified. The room seemed to close in on him, the walls pressing inward, suffocating him with their oppressive presence. He was trapped in a nightmarish loop, where every attempt to escape only led him deeper into the fog of his own mind.

He clutched at his temples, trying to dispel the swirling images and fragmented memories that plagued him. The boundaries between his own perceptions and the reality he sought to uncover had become increasingly blurred. The more he tried to piece together the truth about Emily, the more elusive it seemed.

His eyes darted around the room, searching for some tangible anchor to reality. The remnants of his former life—a framed diploma, a photograph of a happier time—served only as painful reminders of his fall from grace. The stark contrast between his former success and his current state was a cruel irony that gnawed at him.

As he struggled to regain his composure, the weight of his addiction and the burden of his obsession with Emily's case seemed to converge into a single, overwhelming force. He could no longer discern where his memories ended and his hallucinations began. The truth had become a distant, unreachable goal, obscured by the fog of his deteriorating mind.

In a moment of clarity, Henry recalled a crucial detail from his previous visit to the clinic. One of the patients had mentioned a hidden room, a place where the clinic's darkest secrets might be concealed. The patient had spoken in hushed tones, as if afraid of being overheard. The mention of a hidden room had lodged itself in Henry's mind, a fragment of a larger puzzle that he had yet to fully understand.

The idea of a hidden room became an obsession in itself. He envisioned it as a repository of the clinic's secrets, a place where the truth about Emily's disappearance might be locked away. Despite his deteriorating condition, the thought of uncovering this hidden space drove him forward, a flickering beacon in the darkness of his mind.

With a renewed sense of purpose, Henry forced himself to stand, his legs unsteady beneath him. He needed to return to the clinic, to investigate further, and to find the hidden room that might hold the key to unraveling the mystery. He fumbled for his coat and keys, his hands shaking as he prepared to leave.

The chill of the night air hit him like a slap as he stepped outside, the icy wind cutting through his layers of clothing. The streets were eerily quiet, the city's usual bustle replaced by a desolate silence. Henry's breath misted in the cold air, and he struggled to maintain his focus as he made his way back to the clinic.

His journey was marked by a sense of disorientation, the familiar landmarks seeming unfamiliar in the dim light. The fog that had settled over his mind seemed to seep into the world around him, blurring the lines between reality and illusion. He pushed through the disconcerting sensations, driven by a singular goal: to uncover the truth, no matter the cost.

As he approached the clinic, the building loomed before him like a foreboding monolith. The once-imposing structure now appeared even more menacing in the darkness, its cracked and weathered façade a testament to the decay that had set in over the years. Henry's heart raced with a mixture of fear and determination as he entered the building.

The clinic's interior was just as he remembered it: dimly lit and eerily quiet. The oppressive silence was punctuated only by the distant hum of machinery and the occasional creak of the building settling. Henry's footsteps echoed through the corridors as he made his way toward the area where he believed the hidden room might be located.

His mind raced with fragmented memories and distorted perceptions, but he forced himself to concentrate. He retraced his steps from the previous visit, examining the walls and floors for any signs of hidden passages or concealed doors. The search was painstaking and slow, each movement tinged with a growing sense of urgency.

Henry's search led him to a nondescript storage room, its door slightly ajar. The room was filled with dusty medical supplies and old furniture, but Henry's instincts told him that something more significant might be hidden within. He carefully pushed the door open and stepped inside, his eyes scanning the cluttered space.

In the dim light, Henry noticed a small, inconspicuous panel on the wall, partially hidden behind a stack of old medical records. His heart raced as he approached the panel, his hands trembling with a mixture of excitement and apprehension. He carefully pried the panel open, revealing a narrow, dark passageway beyond.

With a deep breath, Henry stepped into the passageway, the darkness enveloping him as he moved forward. The passage was narrow and musty, its walls lined with old, decaying insulation. The air was thick with dust, and Henry's senses were overwhelmed by the oppressive atmosphere.

The passage led to a small, dimly lit room, its contents obscured by shadows. Henry's heart pounded as he stepped inside, his eyes adjusting to the faint light. The room was filled with old filing cabinets and boxes, their contents hidden beneath layers of dust and grime.

Henry approached one of the filing cabinets and carefully opened the drawers, his hands shaking with anticipation.

Inside, he found a collection of old case files and medical records, their contents yellowed with age. He sifted through the files, searching for anything related to Emily Harper or the mysterious disappearances that had plagued the clinic.

As he examined the documents, a sense of unease settled over him. The records revealed a disturbing pattern: several patients had vanished under suspicious circumstances, their cases marked as unresolved. The files were filled with vague notations and incomplete information, as if someone had deliberately sought to obscure the truth.

Henry's hands trembled as he uncovered a file marked "Confidential," its contents neatly organized and meticulously maintained. The file contained detailed records of patients, their treatment plans, and notes on their progress. Among the documents, Henry found a series of notes referencing a covert program designed to handle patients who were deemed "problematic" or "unmanageable."

The notes described a series of procedures and interventions that were supposed to address the needs of these patients, but the language was clinical and devoid of empathy. The program seemed to be a way to control and silence patients who posed a threat to the clinic's reputation or operations.

Henry's mind raced as he absorbed the information. The program described in the notes matched the vague hints and fragmented stories he had heard from the clinic's former patients. It seemed to confirm his suspicions about the clinic's darker activities and its role in the mysterious disappearances.

The documents also contained references to a mysterious benefactor, someone who had funded the clinic's operations and maintained a tight grip on its activities. The name was obscured by redacted information, but the references hinted at a powerful figure with significant influence.

As Henry sifted through the files, he realized that he had stumbled upon a crucial piece of the puzzle. The information contained in the confidential file provided a glimpse into the clinic's hidden agenda and its connection to the broader network of corruption that he had been uncovering. It also reinforced the idea that Emily Harper's disappearance was part of a larger, more sinister scheme.

Despite the overwhelming evidence, Henry felt a growing sense of dread. The more he uncovered, the more he realized how deeply entangled he had become in this web of deception. The lines between reality and hallucination continued to blur, and he struggled to maintain his grip on the truth.

As he prepared to leave the hidden room, Henry's thoughts turned to Emily. The revelations he had uncovered painted a troubling picture of her actions and motivations. The idea that she had faked her disappearance and used him as a pawn in her scheme was both shocking and disheartening.

Henry's mind was a chaotic storm of conflicting emotions. He was driven by a desire to expose the truth, but he was also plagued by doubts and fears. The fog of his addiction and the weight of his own failures threatened to overwhelm him, making it difficult to discern the path forward.

With a final glance at the documents, Henry made his way back through the passageway and emerged into the clinic's main corridor. The oppressive silence of the building seemed even more pronounced in the aftermath of his discovery. He felt a profound sense of isolation, as if he were the only one aware of the dark secrets hidden within these walls.

As he left the clinic and stepped back into the cold night air, Henry was filled with a sense of foreboding. The revelations he had uncovered had only deepened the mystery, and he knew that the path ahead would be fraught with danger and uncertainty. He was driven by a sense of urgency, but he also knew that he needed to confront the truth about Emily and the clinic before it consumed him entirely.

The journey ahead would be treacherous, but Henry was determined to see it through. The truth was within reach, and he was willing to risk everything to uncover it.

The clinic's decrepit corridors echoed with a hollow sound as Henry walked through them, each step heavier than the last. The drug-induced haze that had settled over him in the past few days seemed to lift, if only slightly, as he ventured deeper into the facility. It was as if the very walls of the clinic held the secrets he was desperately seeking.

Henry had spent the last few hours rummaging through the clinic's administrative files, which were kept in a cluttered room filled with stacks of old paperwork and dusty cabinets. The clinic's records were a chaotic jumble of disorganized files and incomplete reports, but Henry's keen eyes had spotted something that had intrigued him: a series of documents buried deep within a cabinet, labeled with ominous tags and marked confidential.

His heart raced as he carefully opened one of the files. Inside were detailed patient records, but what caught his attention were the discrepancies and the patterns of disappearances. Each file had a section marked as "Case Closed," but Henry noticed that many of these cases were marked unresolved or had vague notations suggesting further investigation. The files hinted at something sinister—an overarching conspiracy that seemed to tie the clinic's activities to a larger, more dangerous network.

Henry's hands shook as he leafed through the documents, each page revealing more disturbing details about the clinic's secretive operations. The files included references to a "Special Procedures Program" designed to manage patients who were deemed problematic. These patients were treated with a level of secrecy and detachment that suggested something beyond mere therapeutic intervention.

As he sifted through the papers, Henry's mind raced with the implications. The Special Procedures Program seemed to be a euphemism for something far more nefarious—possibly a method of silencing patients or controlling them through unethical means. The notes were clinical and devoid of empathy, focusing on methods of containment rather than treatment. This realization sent a chill down his spine.

Henry's thoughts then turned to Emily Harper. The more he read, the more it became apparent that she was not the only one affected by this dark aspect of the clinic. The pattern of disappearances aligned with her case—vague notations, missing information, and a lack of follow-up. It was as if Emily's disappearance was part of a larger, systemic problem within the clinic.

With mounting urgency, Henry pulled out a detailed case file labeled with Emily's name. It was thicker than the others and contained a comprehensive record of her treatment, interactions with the clinic staff, and her progress. As he flipped through the pages, he found evidence of her deteriorating mental state, but there were also hints of something more—a pattern of interventions that seemed more punitive than therapeutic.

Henry's eyes widened as he found a note scribbled in the margins of one of Emily's treatment records. The note referred to a meeting with a high-level administrator and mentioned a decision to "take further action." It was a cryptic message, but it suggested that there had been a significant, possibly covert, decision made about Emily's treatment.

The pieces began to fall into place. The clinic's actions were not just about treating patients; they were about controlling them, silencing them, and manipulating them for unknown reasons. Emily's disappearance seemed to be a direct result of this insidious program—a program that Henry had inadvertently become entangled in.

As he continued to study the documents, Henry's thoughts were interrupted by a sudden, piercing pain in his head. His addiction had left him vulnerable, and the pressure of uncovering such a troubling conspiracy was taking its toll. He gripped the edge of the desk, trying to steady himself, but the room seemed to spin.

Taking a deep breath, Henry forced himself to focus. He needed to get out of the clinic and regroup. The information he had uncovered was critical, but it was also overwhelming. He had to piece together the fragments of truth and make sense of the larger picture.

With great effort, Henry gathered the files and placed them in a folder. He carefully secured the folder in his bag, knowing that this information was crucial to understanding the full scope of the conspiracy. As he made his way out of the clinic, he felt a mix of dread and determination. The path ahead was fraught with danger, but he was driven by a sense of purpose.

The fog of his addiction seemed to lift slightly as he left the clinic and stepped into the cold night air. The city was quiet, and the darkness of the night seemed to mirror the uncertainty and danger that lay ahead. Henry knew that he was on the brink of uncovering something significant, but he also knew that the truth came with a heavy price.

He needed to confront the reality of the clinic's operations and Emily's role in it. The evidence suggested that Emily's disappearance was part of a larger scheme, and he had to determine whether she was a victim or an active participant in this dark narrative. The burden of truth was heavy, but Henry was determined to see it through.

As he walked away from the clinic, Henry's mind raced with the implications of what he had discovered. The pieces of the puzzle were falling into place, but the picture was still incomplete. He knew that he needed more information to fully understand the extent of the conspiracy and Emily's involvement in it.

The city's lights flickered in the distance as Henry made his way back to his apartment. The chill in the air was a stark contrast to the warmth of the clinic's hidden rooms. He felt a sense of urgency as he contemplated his next steps. He needed to find more clues, more evidence, and possibly allies who could help him unravel the mystery.

Henry's thoughts turned to the recovering addicts he had met at the clinic. They had hinted at something dark lurking within the facility, but their reluctance to speak openly had left him with more questions than answers. He resolved to return to them, to seek out more information and to understand the full scope of the clinic's operations.

As he entered his apartment, Henry's mind was a whirlwind of thoughts and emotions. The revelations about the clinic had left him shaken, but they had also given him a renewed sense of purpose. He was determined to uncover the truth, no matter the cost.

He sat down at his cluttered desk, the flickering light of a single lamp casting long shadows across the room. The documents he had retrieved from the clinic lay in front of him, and he began to sift through them once more. Each page was a piece of a larger puzzle, and he needed to connect the dots to reveal the full extent of the conspiracy.

The clock ticked loudly in the silence of the room, marking the passage of time as Henry delved deeper into the files. The information was overwhelming, but he was driven by a sense of urgency and determination. The truth about Emily and the clinic was within reach, and he was committed to uncovering it.

As the hours passed, Henry's exhaustion began to take its toll. His mind was foggy, and the weight of the information was becoming increasingly difficult to bear. But he pressed on, driven by the belief that he was on the brink of a breakthrough.

With a final glance at the documents, Henry knew that the journey ahead would be fraught with challenges and dangers. But he was ready to face whatever lay ahead, driven by the desire to uncover the truth and to find answers to the questions that had plagued him for so long.

Chapter 5: The Addicts' Circle

The neon sign flickered intermittently outside the decrepit building, casting an unsteady glow on the rain-soaked sidewalk. Henry Talbot stood under the awning, his fingers nervously drumming against his thigh. The weight of his addiction pressed heavily on his shoulders, a constant reminder of the shattered life he'd led. But tonight, it was not the alcohol or the amphetamines that consumed him. It was the urgency to find answers about Emily Harper, the missing piece in his fractured life.

Inside, the clinic was dimly lit and smelled faintly of antiseptic and stale coffee. Henry's footsteps echoed off the bare walls as he walked through the lobby, the décor a faded testament to better days long past. The air was thick with the scent of desperation and hope—a fitting ambiance for what he was about to undertake.

He was here to attend a secret support group for recovering addicts, a place that had become a crucible of truth in his search for Emily. According to his sources, it was here that he might find the missing links to her past. Henry approached the front desk where a weary receptionist greeted him with a forced smile.

"I'm here for the support group," Henry said, his voice rough and strained.

The receptionist, a middle-aged woman with tired eyes, handed him a visitor's badge. "Down the hall, second door on your left. The group's already started."

Henry nodded, slipping the badge into his pocket, and made his way to the meeting room. The door creaked open to reveal a circle of chairs arranged around a single, small table. A handful of people, their faces gaunt and tired, looked up at him with varying degrees of curiosity and indifference.

The room was silent save for the soft hum of an old air conditioner. Henry took a seat at the back, his presence barely acknowledged by the group. He was an outsider here, a mere observer in a place where secrets were shared and demons were faced.

The group facilitator, a woman named Linda with an air of quiet authority, spoke gently but firmly. Her voice carried a tone of understanding that Henry found oddly comforting. She guided the group through a series of sharing exercises, encouraging each member to talk about their struggles and progress.

As the session continued, Henry listened intently. He heard stories of battles with addiction, of lives derailed by substances and circumstances. Each narrative was a thread in the larger tapestry of pain and redemption that bound these individuals together.

His attention was drawn to a young woman sitting across from him. Mia, as she introduced herself, had an air of quiet intensity. Her dark eyes, though haunted, were sharp and observant. She spoke with a raw honesty that caught Henry's interest.

"I was in rehab here a year ago," Mia said, her voice steady despite the tremor in her hands. "I knew Emily Harper. She was one of the patients who came and went quickly, always seemed like she was looking for something."

Henry's heart quickened. This was the lead he had been waiting for. He leaned forward slightly, trying to catch every word.

"What was she like?" he asked, his voice barely above a whisper.

Mia glanced around the room, as if ensuring no one was eavesdropping, before continuing. "Emily was... troubled. More than the others. She had this way of talking about her life like it was a script she was trying to rewrite. It wasn't just about the addiction for her. There was a whole other layer."

Henry's mind raced. This was consistent with what he remembered—Emily had always seemed like she was hiding something deeper, a secret buried beneath her outward struggles.

"She used to talk about someone controlling her, someone she feared," Mia said, her gaze locking onto Henry's. "She mentioned Simon Harper often. There were whispers that she was trying to escape him, that he was the real problem."

Henry's pulse raced. Simon Harper—the name was like a dark cloud hanging over his investigation. If Emily had been trying to escape Simon, it only deepened the mystery of her disappearance. Henry leaned in closer, his voice laced with urgency.

"Do you know why she disappeared so suddenly?" he asked. "Was she planning to leave? Did she say anything about her plans?"

Mia's expression grew pensive. "She never gave a lot away. But there was a sense that she was planning something drastic. I remember one night she was talking about leaving everything behind—her old life, her problems, and even the clinic."

Henry felt a surge of hope mixed with dread. If Emily had planned to disappear, it could mean that she was still out there, hiding. But it also raised new questions: Why had she left? And how had Simon Harper played into all of this?

As the session came to a close, Linda announced a break. The group members dispersed, some heading for the refreshments table while others retreated into quieter corners of the room. Henry approached Mia cautiously, his mind buzzing with questions.

"Mia, can we talk?" he asked, his voice low and earnest.

Mia hesitated for a moment before nodding. "Sure. But let's keep it quick. I don't want to draw too much attention."

They moved to a quieter part of the clinic, a small lounge area cluttered with old magazines and worn-out furniture. Henry took a seat on a frayed couch, watching as Mia sat down across from him.

"Why are you so interested in Emily Harper?" Mia asked, her tone a mix of curiosity and caution.

Henry's eyes met hers. "Emily was my patient. She disappeared, and I'm trying to find out what happened to her. Her case has haunted me."

Mia's gaze softened with sympathy. "I understand. But you should know, Emily was not the easiest person to deal with. She had a lot of issues, and she could be manipulative. She wanted people to believe her story, but sometimes the truth was different."

Henry's heart sank. He had suspected as much, but hearing it confirmed was another blow. "What do you mean by 'manipulative'? How did she use people?"

Mia took a deep breath, choosing her words carefully. "Emily had this ability to play people. She could make you feel like you were the only person who understood her, but it was all a part of her act. She had a way of making you think that her problems were your fault, that you were responsible for fixing them."

Henry felt a pang of self-reproach. Had he been a pawn in Emily's game all along? He shook his head, trying to clear the thoughts. "Did she ever mention anyone else who might have been involved in her life or disappearance?"

Mia's eyes narrowed thoughtfully. "There was one name she mentioned occasionally—Simon Harper. She spoke of him as if he was a shadow over her life. I don't know the details, but there was a sense that he was the source of her fears."

Henry's mind raced. Simon Harper was the key to unraveling this entire mess. If Emily had been trying to escape Simon, then he was undoubtedly a significant part of her story.

"Do you have any idea where Emily might have gone after she left the clinic?" Henry asked.

Mia shook her head. "I wish I did. But she left abruptly. No one knew where she went, and it was like she vanished into thin air."

Henry felt a mixture of frustration and determination. Emily's disappearance was becoming increasingly tangled, but the clues he had gathered were leading him closer to the truth.

"Thank you, Mia," Henry said sincerely. "Your information has been helpful. If you think of anything else, please let me know."

Mia nodded. "I will. Just be careful. Emily's world was messy and dangerous. You might find yourself in deeper trouble than you expect."

As Henry left the clinic, the weight of Mia's words pressed heavily on his shoulders. Emily's manipulation, Simon's dark influence, and the mystery of her disappearance were all converging into a web of deceit and danger. Henry knew that the answers he sought were within his grasp, but the path ahead was fraught with peril.

Walking back to his apartment, the night air was cold and biting. Henry's thoughts churned with the revelations from the support group. He had come closer to understanding Emily's disappearance, but the road ahead was still shrouded in darkness.

He knew that the next step in his investigation would be critical. To uncover the full truth about Emily, he would have to delve deeper into Simon Harper's life and connections. The clues were scattered, but Henry was determined to piece them together, no matter the cost.

Henry sat in the dimly lit room of the recovering addicts' support group, feeling a mixture of anticipation and unease. The small, windowless space smelled faintly of stale coffee and cigarette smoke. He was surrounded by a mix of faces—some with weary eyes, others with an unnerving intensity. Each one had their own story, their own battle scars. Henry had managed to convince them that he was there to seek help, but in reality, he was there to pry into their pasts.

Mia was sitting across from him, her slender fingers wrapped tightly around a coffee mug. Her face was marked with a blend of tiredness and defiance. She had been one of the more open members of the group, which is why Henry had been drawn to her. She had spoken about Emily with a degree of familiarity that intrigued him. Her presence here, coupled with the cryptic comment about Emily's connection to Simon, made her a critical piece of the puzzle.

Henry leaned forward, his voice low and measured. "Mia, you mentioned something the other day about Emily planning to escape. Can you elaborate on that? And what did you mean about Simon?"

Mia's eyes flitted nervously around the room before settling back on Henry. Her posture shifted slightly as if bracing for impact. "Emily wasn't just any patient. She was smart—more clever than most gave her credit for. During her time here, she talked about getting out, about starting a new life. She had this look in her eyes, like she was preparing for a big change."

Henry listened intently, his heart pounding. This was the first real lead he had gotten in weeks. "Did she ever say anything about Simon, her husband?"

Mia hesitated, biting her lip. "She didn't talk about him much, but she did mention that he was controlling, abusive. She was scared of him. More than once, she said that if she stayed with him, she'd lose her mind. But there was something else, something more... sinister."

Henry's curiosity deepened. "Sinister? What do you mean?"

Mia took a deep breath. "There were times when I'd see Emily talking to herself or making secretive phone calls. She was always worried that someone was watching her. It was like she was involved in something dangerous, but she never told anyone the full story."

Henry's mind raced. If Emily was preparing to escape, it meant she had a plan, a strategy. The notion that she had something planned against Simon—and possibly against Henry—was both chilling and intriguing. "Did she ever talk about her plans directly to you or anyone else?"

"Not directly," Mia admitted. "But one time, she let slip that she was in touch with someone who was helping her with her plans. She mentioned a name, but I couldn't catch it clearly. It sounded like a contact she trusted."

Henry's thoughts swirled. Emily had a contact—a third party who might have been aiding her escape. Could this person be linked to Simon or, more disturbingly, to the corruption he suspected within the rehab center?

Before Henry could probe further, a man entered the room—a tall, broad-shouldered figure with an air of authority. The meeting was about to start. Henry's window to interrogate Mia was closing fast. He flashed her a pleading look. "Mia, is there any way I can contact you outside of this group? I need to follow up on this."

Mia's eyes softened, and she nodded. "I'll give you my number. But be careful. There are things you don't know, and some people might not want you digging around."

As the group's facilitator began the meeting, Henry took a moment to process what he had just learned. Mia's information provided him with a thread to pull, but he had to be cautious. The labyrinthine nature of Emily's plans and the shadowy connections he was uncovering could lead him into dangerous territory.

Later that night, back in his dingy apartment, Henry stared at the crumpled piece of paper where Mia had scrawled her number. The room was cloaked in darkness, lit only by the flickering light of a solitary lamp. The walls seemed to close in on him, amplifying the sense of isolation that had become his constant companion.

Henry's mind raced through the implications of Mia's revelations. Emily's escape plan, her fear of Simon, and the mysterious contact she had mentioned all pointed to a larger conspiracy. If Emily had orchestrated her disappearance to frame Simon, it would explain the disarray in his own life—the professional ruin, the emotional wreckage. But it also raised disturbing questions about his own role in her plan.

Was he merely a pawn in Emily's scheme, manipulated by her vulnerability and desperation? Or was there a deeper connection between Emily's disappearance and the shadowy network of corruption within the mental health system?

Henry needed to find out more about Emily's contact. If Mia could provide him with a name, it might lead him closer to understanding the full scope of Emily's plans. He decided to meet with Mia again, outside of the support group setting, where they could talk more freely.

The next day, Henry arranged to meet Mia at a small café on the edge of town. The establishment was quaint, a stark contrast to the grimy environments Henry had become accustomed to. As he waited at a corner table, he observed the patrons around him—young couples, businesspeople, and elderly individuals enjoying their meals. The normalcy of the place felt like a strange sanctuary from his turbulent reality.

Mia arrived shortly, her appearance more composed than the night before. She slid into the seat opposite Henry, her eyes scanning the café before settling on him. "Sorry for the wait," she said, offering a faint smile. "I had some things to take care of."

Henry nodded, his expression serious. "Thank you for meeting me. I need more information about Emily's contact—anything you remember."

Mia glanced around, ensuring their conversation was private. "I remember one name she mentioned—Lena. Lena something. It wasn't clear, but it was definitely a woman. Emily seemed to trust her a lot."

"Lena," Henry repeated, his mind already racing. "Do you know where I might find this Lena?"

Mia shook her head. "I don't know much else. Emily was careful not to reveal too much. But I think Lena might be connected to the clinic or maybe someone outside of it who was helping her."

Henry took out a notepad and jotted down the name. Lena. It was a lead, a potential link to uncovering the truth behind Emily's disappearance and her manipulation of his life.

"Thank you, Mia," Henry said, his voice tinged with gratitude. "I'll follow up on this. I appreciate your help."

Mia's eyes held a glint of concern. "Be careful, Henry. There's a lot more to this than you realize. Some things are better left uncovered."

As Mia left the café, Henry felt a renewed sense of determination. Lena could be the key to unraveling the web of deceit surrounding Emily and Simon. The path ahead was fraught with danger and uncertainty, but Henry was driven by a relentless need for truth and redemption.

With the name Lena now in his possession, Henry knew his next steps would be crucial. He had to find out who Lena was, what role she played in Emily's life, and how she might be connected to the larger conspiracy he was slowly piecing together.

As he left the café, Henry's thoughts turned to his dwindling resources and the mounting risks. His addiction still clawed at him, and his finances were stretched thin. But the prospect of uncovering the truth about Emily—and, ultimately, clearing his own name—gave him a renewed sense of purpose.

Henry walked through the bustling streets of the city, the weight of his mission pressing heavily on his shoulders. The path ahead was uncertain, but he was resolute. Lena was the next piece of the puzzle, and he would do whatever it took to find her and uncover the truth behind Emily's disappearance.

Chapter 6: The Hunt for Simon

Dr. Henry Talbot had always envisioned himself as a man of reason and control, guiding others through their darkest moments with the precision of a skilled surgeon. Yet, standing on the doorstep of Simon Harper's new residence, he felt the stark reality of his own unraveling life pressing heavily on his shoulders. The crisp autumn air did little to alleviate the oppressive weight of his mission. Simon had moved on, reestablishing himself far from the wreckage that had once defined their professional and personal lives. Henry's fingers trembled slightly as he knocked on the door, each rap echoing his internal torment.

The door creaked open to reveal a well-groomed middle-aged man with a stoic expression. Simon's eyes flicked over Henry with a mixture of curiosity and disdain. "Henry Talbot," Simon said, his voice steady but carrying an undercurrent of surprise. "I didn't expect to see you here."

Henry took a deep breath, struggling to maintain his composure. "Simon, we need to talk. It's about Emily."

Simon's expression hardened, and he glanced back into the house as if considering whether to slam the door shut. After a moment, he stepped aside and gestured for Henry to enter. The interior was a stark contrast to Henry's dingy apartment—tasteful, immaculate, a reflection of Simon's new life. Simon led Henry into a sitting room adorned with expensive furniture and an array of framed certificates and accolades.

Simon motioned for Henry to sit, but he remained standing, his posture rigid. Henry slumped into an armchair, feeling the weight of Simon's scrutiny. "I've been following your recent activities," Simon said, his voice edged with a touch of amusement. "Seems you've become quite the detective."

Henry stared at Simon, the image of Emily's fearful face flashing in his mind. "I know you're involved in her disappearance. I have proof that ties you to the clinic and to Emily's case."

Simon's face tightened. "Proof? Henry, I haven't been involved in Emily's life for years. I've moved on. I suggest you do the same."

Henry stood up abruptly, frustration and anger bubbling over. "You're lying, Simon. Emily was terrified of you. She came to me for help, and then she vanished. You have a history of control and manipulation."

Simon's eyes narrowed dangerously. "You have no idea what you're talking about. Emily was unstable, Henry. Her disappearance had nothing to do with me."

Henry's mind raced, struggling to piece together Simon's words and actions. "The clinic, the shady dealings—there's a pattern, Simon. I need to know the truth."

Simon's expression remained impassive. "You're grasping at straws, Henry. If you're so convinced of my involvement, why not take it up with the authorities? But remember, accusations without evidence can be dangerous."

The conversation was spiraling, and Henry could feel his grip on the situation slipping. Simon's calm demeanor was maddening, and Henry's frustration was mounting. "I know what I've seen," Henry said, his voice shaking. "And I know you're hiding something."

Simon walked to the door, signaling that the conversation was over. "Leave now, Henry. Before you make things worse for yourself. I won't be dragged into your mess."

Henry hesitated, feeling the sting of Simon's dismissal. He turned to leave, casting one last glance over his shoulder. "This isn't over, Simon. I'll find the truth, even if it means uncovering your darkest secrets."

As Henry stepped out into the brisk air, he felt a mix of anger and doubt. Simon's denial had only deepened the mystery. The confrontation had yielded little tangible evidence but had provided a new perspective—Simon's manipulation and cold detachment were indicative of a deeper game.

Henry walked back to his car, his mind a swirl of conflicting emotions. The confrontation had left him unsettled, and the weight of Simon's words gnawed at him. Was Simon truly innocent, or was he playing a role in a much larger and more sinister scheme?

Henry's drive back to his apartment was fraught with agitation. The familiar streets of his old neighborhood seemed different, tainted by the shadows of his investigation. He parked his car and sat for a moment, staring at the cracked pavement and the flickering streetlights. The world outside felt distorted, reflecting the chaos in his mind.

As he stumbled into his apartment, the oppressive silence greeted him. The dim light of his living room did little to alleviate the heaviness that had settled over him. He reached for the bottle of whiskey that had become his constant companion, seeking solace in its numbing embrace.

Sitting in his worn armchair, Henry tried to make sense of the day's events. Simon's words echoed in his mind, and Henry grappled with the growing sense of paranoia and doubt. Was he chasing ghosts, or was there a hidden truth waiting to be uncovered?

The answer seemed elusive, and Henry's thoughts turned inward. He recalled the evidence he had amassed, the whispers of corruption, and the disjointed fragments of Emily's story. Each piece of the puzzle seemed to shift, the lines between reality and delusion blurring.

As the hours passed, Henry's exhaustion deepened. The bottle of whiskey stood empty beside him, and the haze of alcohol began to take its toll. Sleep came in fragmented bursts, filled with troubling dreams that reflected his inner turmoil. Shadows danced on the walls, and whispers of Emily's voice mingled with distorted images of Simon's face.

When morning arrived, Henry awoke to find himself tangled in the remnants of his own despair. The remnants of his dreams lingered, casting an uneasy pall over the day. He needed to refocus, to find clarity amidst the chaos.

Henry's next move was clear: he needed to dig deeper into Simon's past and present connections. The confrontation had not yielded the answers he sought, but it had underscored the necessity of further investigation. Simon's denial was a defense, and Henry had to find a way to break through it.

Determined, Henry set out to trace Simon's recent activities. He began by reviewing old files and news reports related to Simon's business ventures and public appearances. There had to be something—an overlooked detail or an unreported connection—that could offer insight into Simon's true role in Emily's disappearance.

As he delved into the research, Henry discovered a pattern of philanthropy and business investments that Simon had maintained since Emily's disappearance. Charitable donations, high-profile events, and strategic alliances painted a picture of a man who had successfully rebranded himself. The clean image Simon projected was at odds with the dark undertones Henry had unearthed.

One particular investment caught Henry's attention—a new venture that Simon had recently funded, which focused on mental health and addiction treatment. The timing was suspicious, and Henry couldn't help but wonder if it was a calculated move to divert attention from his past misdeeds.

Henry's investigation led him to contact former colleagues and acquaintances of Simon, hoping to gather additional information. Each conversation added a layer to the complex web of Simon's public persona and private dealings. The more Henry learned, the clearer it became that Simon had orchestrated a masterful reinvention, distancing himself from the controversies of the past.

Despite his mounting evidence, Henry felt increasingly isolated. The confrontation with Simon had left him with more questions than answers, and the path forward was shrouded in uncertainty. The journey to uncover the truth was taking a toll on his already fragile state of mind.

As the days wore on, Henry's search for answers became an all-consuming obsession. The lines between his personal quest and professional failure blurred, and the strain began to manifest in his behavior. His addiction worsened, and the brief moments of clarity he experienced became increasingly rare.

Henry's focus shifted to finding concrete evidence that would expose Simon's involvement. The task was daunting, but he felt driven by a sense of justice and a desperate need to validate his own experiences. He knew that uncovering the truth was the only way to reclaim some semblance of control over his life.

In the midst of his investigation, Henry found a glimmer of hope in a lead that suggested Simon's connections to influential figures in the mental health industry. If he could establish a direct link between Simon and the corruption Henry suspected, it could unravel the entire network.

Determined to pursue this lead, Henry prepared for a new phase of his investigation. He knew that the journey ahead would be fraught with challenges and risks, but he was resolved to see it through. The search for the truth had become not just a quest for justice but a personal crusade to redeem himself from the ruins of his past.

As he set out to follow this new lead, Henry was acutely aware of the dangers that lay ahead. The pursuit of truth was a treacherous path, and the shadows of his own history loomed large. Yet, despite the uncertainties and the mounting pressure, Henry remained resolute. The hunt for Simon Harper had only just begun, and the answers he sought were tantalizingly close.

Henry stumbled into his dingy apartment, his head throbbing from a combination of the alcohol he had downed and the drugs that had left him feeling like he was floating in a murky dream. The confrontation with Simon Harper had left him reeling, but not from the physical confrontation alone; it was Simon's calculated denials and his portrayal of Emily as an unstable woman that gnawed at Henry's sanity.

The cold light of dawn was seeping through the grimy windows, casting a sallow hue over the room. Henry collapsed onto his threadbare couch, the remnants of his once-pristine suit crumpling beneath him. He stared at the wall, the stains and peeling wallpaper a stark reminder of how far he had fallen from his former life. His mind was a chaos of fragmented thoughts, struggling to piece together the shattered puzzle of his past.

Simon had painted a picture of Emily that seemed almost too convenient. He claimed she was a deeply troubled woman, prone to delusions and manipulative schemes. At first, Henry had dismissed it as Simon's attempt to deflect guilt. But now, doubt began to creep in. What if Simon was right? What if Emily had indeed been a master manipulator, using her charm and vulnerability to exploit those around her?

Henry's grip tightened around the bottle of bourbon he had been nursing. He took another swig, the fiery liquid burning down his throat, attempting to drown out the rising tide of paranoia that threatened to overwhelm him. The room spun slightly as he tried to focus, his eyes landing on the scattered papers and therapy notes strewn across his coffee table.

He picked up a worn file, one of the many he had retrieved from the back of his closet. The documents were old, filled with details about Emily's therapy sessions, her complaints about Simon, and her bouts of anxiety. Each page seemed to blur into the next, and the lines between reality and delusion began to dissolve.

Henry's head fell back against the couch, and he closed his eyes, trying to sift through his jumbled memories. His thoughts were disjointed, a jumble of half-remembered conversations and distorted recollections. The more he thought about Emily's past, the more he began to doubt his own perceptions. Had he misinterpreted her fears? Was he the one who had been manipulated?

The memories of their sessions were hazy, distorted by time and his substance abuse. He recalled Emily's tearful admissions, her desperate pleas for help, and her complaints about Simon's controlling behavior. But now, he questioned if those were genuine cries for help or if they were part of a carefully crafted act designed to elicit sympathy and manipulate those around her.

In a desperate bid to ground himself, Henry grabbed the stack of notes and began to sift through them, trying to find something, anything, that would make sense of the chaos swirling in his mind. He flipped through the pages, skimming over the repetitive phrases and emotional outbursts until he came across a note he had marked with a red pen.

It was a session summary where Emily had spoken of her fear of Simon's retaliation. She had mentioned feeling trapped, cornered, and threatened. The urgency in her voice had been palpable, but now, as Henry read the words again, he wondered if he had been too quick to accept them at face value. Had he been blinded by his own feelings of inadequacy and guilt?

Henry's thoughts were interrupted by a loud knock on the door. Startled, he stumbled up, the room spinning around him. He opened the door to find a delivery man holding a package, a large envelope marked with the clinic's logo. Henry's heart raced as he took the envelope, feeling an uneasy sense of foreboding.

Inside, he found a folder filled with documents from the clinic. It was as if someone had deliberately sent him these papers to provoke him. Henry's hands trembled as he leafed through the contents, which included patient records, internal memos, and financial statements. One document in particular caught his eye: a ledger detailing significant payments made to a mysterious third party.

The name of the benefactor was not immediately clear, but the payments were frequent and substantial. Henry's paranoia flared as he tried to make sense of the information. Was this evidence of a larger conspiracy, or was it another layer of manipulation designed to keep him off balance?

His mind raced as he considered the possibility that Emily might have been involved in this shadowy network. Was she part of a scheme to exploit vulnerable individuals for financial gain? Could she have been a pawn in a game far more complex than he had initially realized?

Henry's paranoia deepened as he realized that the network he was uncovering might be intertwined with his own downfall. His career had been destroyed by the scandal surrounding Emily, and now it seemed that the very system he had once been a part of was corrupt to its core. The thought that Emily might have been an orchestrator in this conspiracy, using him as a means to an end, was almost too much to bear.

In his state of confusion, Henry's sense of reality became increasingly tenuous. The line between truth and delusion blurred, and he found himself questioning every interaction, every piece of evidence, and every memory he had of Emily.

Was she a victim of a corrupt system, or was she a manipulative force in her own right?

As the days passed, Henry's obsession with the case grew more consuming. He began to isolate himself further, pushing away those who tried to help him. His addiction worsened, and his attempts to connect the dots between Emily's disappearance and the clinic's corruption seemed more desperate and disconnected.

He continued to revisit the clinic, hoping to find answers amidst the wreckage of his past. The former patients he spoke to seemed to sense his growing instability, their responses increasingly guarded and wary. It was as if the clinic's toxic environment had seeped into every aspect of his investigation, leaving him trapped in a web of deceit and paranoia.

One evening, Henry received a phone call from Mia, the recovering addict he had met earlier. Her voice was tense, and she spoke in hurried, fragmented sentences. "Henry, you need to be careful. There's more to this than you know. I think Emily's connected to something bigger—something dangerous."

Henry's heart raced as he listened to Mia's words. He asked her to meet him at a nearby diner, hoping that her insight could help him piece together the remaining fragments of his investigation. When she arrived, her expression was one of deep concern, and she handed Henry a manila envelope.

Inside, he found more documents related to the clinic's financial dealings and a note scrawled in shaky handwriting: "Follow the money. You're not seeing the whole picture. Emily is more involved than you think."

The cryptic message only deepened Henry's sense of paranoia. Was Mia trying to help him, or was she part of a scheme to manipulate him further? As he examined the documents, he noticed a series of transactions linked to a network of shell companies and anonymous donors.

Henry's mind raced as he considered the implications. The network of corruption he was uncovering seemed to be more extensive than he had anticipated, with ties reaching into the city's elite. The thought that Emily might have been orchestrating this grand scheme, using him and others as pawns, was overwhelming.

In a fit of desperation, Henry returned to his apartment and began to scour the documents for any clue that might make sense of the chaos. His addiction-fueled paranoia reached its peak as he confronted his own shattered memories and questioned the very nature of his reality.

He was alone, surrounded by the remnants of his former life, grappling with the horrifying realization that Emily might have been a calculating manipulator all along. The thought of her exploiting his vulnerability and using him to further her own agenda left him feeling utterly betrayed and isolated.

As the days blurred into one another, Henry's descent into paranoia continued unabated. He was haunted by the specters of his past and the growing realization that the truth he sought might be more elusive and devastating than he had ever imagined. The final pieces of the puzzle seemed just out of reach, taunting him with the promise of clarity while shrouding him in darkness.

The hunt for Simon and the elusive benefactor behind the clinic's corruption was becoming a personal nightmare, and

Henry's grip on reality slipped further with each passing day. His once-clear mission to uncover the truth now seemed entangled in a web of deceit and manipulation, leaving him to question if he would ever find redemption—or if he was doomed to be consumed by the very darkness he sought to expose.

Chapter 7: Dark Connections

The discovery was both thrilling and terrifying. The network of corruption Henry was piecing together was vast and deeply embedded in the city's most powerful circles. As he waded through the tangled web of deceit, he found himself plunging into a dark abyss that seemed to have no bottom.

It started with the cryptic file he had found hidden in the clinic's basement—an old ledger detailing transactions, names, and dates that seemed insignificant at first. The ledger had led him to financial records that suggested the clinic was more than just a place for addiction treatment. It was a hub of illicit activities, a front for a more sinister operation. Henry had always suspected that something was amiss, but the evidence he had uncovered now confirmed his darkest fears.

The next step was to trace the connections between the clinic and Simon Harper's business dealings. Henry found himself in a dingy office on the edge of town, poring over legal documents and financial statements. The office belonged to a small-time accountant who had once worked for Simon. The accountant, a gaunt man named Leonard, was nervous as he shuffled through stacks of paperwork.

"This isn't my usual line of work," Leonard said, his voice trembling. "I just did the books. Simon's the one who handled all the big deals."

Henry scanned the documents spread out before him. They detailed numerous transactions between Simon's companies and the clinic. The amounts were staggering, and the timing of the transactions raised red flags. It was clear that Simon had been funneling money into the clinic, but what was even more troubling was the pattern of payments. They seemed to coincide with the disappearances of several patients, including Emily.

Leonard's eyes darted around the room. "I don't know much about what went on behind the scenes. All I know is that Simon was always very secretive about his dealings. He paid well, but he didn't tolerate questions."

Henry leaned closer, his mind racing. "What can you tell me about the people Simon was involved with? Any names, addresses?"

Leonard hesitated, but then reluctantly handed over a folder containing names and contact details. "These are some of the people Simon was connected to. They're influential in high society, but I don't know much else."

Henry flipped through the folder. The names were a who's who of the city's elite, including politicians, business magnates, and high-ranking officials. It was clear that Simon had built a network of powerful allies, and the clinic was a key part of this network.

Armed with this new information, Henry began to dig deeper into the connections. He discovered that the clinic's board of directors included several prominent figures who had also been involved in questionable activities. The more he uncovered, the more he realized that Emily's disappearance was just one piece of a much larger puzzle.

Henry's investigation led him to a series of confidential reports that detailed how the clinic had been used to control and silence individuals who were seen as threats to the network's operations. Patients who became too vocal or who threatened to expose the clinic's activities were often manipulated into silence or, in some cases, simply disappeared.

As he reviewed these reports, Henry's mind was overwhelmed by the enormity of the conspiracy. The realization that Emily's case was not an isolated incident but part of a larger pattern of exploitation and corruption was both sobering and infuriating. He felt a growing sense of urgency to bring this information to light, but he knew that doing so would put him at risk.

Henry decided to approach a journalist who had a reputation for investigating corruption. Evelyn Carter was known for her fearless reporting on scandals and her ability to connect disparate pieces of information. Henry hoped that she could help him make sense of the evidence and expose the network's crimes.

He arranged a meeting with Evelyn at a small café on the outskirts of the city. As he waited for her to arrive, Henry's nerves were on edge. The café was a quiet place, far from the prying eyes of the city's elite, but Henry couldn't shake the feeling that he was being watched.

When Evelyn arrived, she was sharp and professional, her demeanor reflecting years of experience in the field. She listened intently as Henry outlined his findings, his voice tinged with desperation.

"This is a significant amount of evidence," Evelyn said, reviewing the documents Henry had brought. "If what you're saying is true, this could be the biggest scandal the city has seen in years."

Henry nodded. "I believe Emily was part of a scheme to expose this network. She might have faked her disappearance to get out of her marriage and frame Simon, but the network's corruption goes far beyond her case."

Evelyn's eyes narrowed as she considered the implications. "We'll need to verify these claims and gather more evidence. If this is as big as you say, it could be dangerous."

Henry understood the risks involved. He had already experienced the dangerous side of this investigation, but the thought of bringing the network's corruption into the light of day gave him a renewed sense of purpose. He was determined to see this through, even if it meant putting himself in harm's way.

Over the following days, Henry and Evelyn worked tirelessly to gather more evidence. They interviewed former patients of the clinic, tracked down additional financial records, and reached out to other journalists who had covered similar cases. The more they uncovered, the more they realized how deep the corruption ran.

Henry's obsession with the case continued to consume him. His addiction worsened, and he found himself spiraling into a state of paranoia. He was convinced that the network was watching his every move, and he became increasingly paranoid about who he could trust. Evelyn remained his anchor, but even her presence couldn't completely dispel the fear that gnawed at him.

One night, as Henry sat alone in his apartment, he received an anonymous phone call. The voice on the other end was distorted, but the message was clear: "Stop digging, or you'll find out just how deep this rabbit hole goes."

The threat was a chilling reminder of the danger he was facing. But Henry refused to be intimidated. He knew that exposing the network's corruption was his only chance at redemption and at finding the truth about Emily.

As Henry and Evelyn continued their investigation, they started to piece together a clearer picture of the network's operations. They discovered that the clinic was a key player in a larger scheme involving illegal drug trafficking, human trafficking, and other criminal activities. The network had used its influence to keep these activities hidden from the public eye, and the clinic had been a crucial part of their operation.

Henry's investigation had uncovered a dark and powerful conspiracy, but he was still left with many unanswered questions. What had happened to Emily after her disappearance? Had she managed to escape the network's clutches, or was she still a pawn in their twisted game?

As he grappled with these questions, Henry's own sanity continued to erode. His addiction clouded his judgment, and he found it increasingly difficult to separate reality from his hallucinations. The line between his obsession with Emily and his own deteriorating mental state grew increasingly blurred.

Despite the mounting pressure and the threats against him, Henry pressed on. He knew that the truth about the network and Emily's disappearance was out there, and he was determined to uncover it, no matter the cost.

Henry Talbot's nights had become a blur of sleeplessness and paranoia. Each evening, after another draining day of searching for answers, he would find himself sprawled across his grimy couch, surrounded by crumpled notes and half-empty bottles of whiskey. But tonight, the dismal routine was interrupted by a new sense of urgency. The financial records he'd obtained were more than just numbers; they were the threads connecting a vast web of corruption. His next steps had to be calculated with precision.

Henry's fingertips trembled as he pored over the documents spread out before him. The small apartment he had once called his sanctuary was now a chaotic crime scene of his own making, cluttered with case files, bank statements, and scribbled notes. The walls seemed to close in on him, suffocating him with the oppressive weight of his own obsession. But the numbers on the page spoke of a more insidious reality, and Henry was determined to unravel it.

The papers revealed a complex network of financial transactions linking the clinic to Simon Harper's business ventures. Each transaction was a clue, a breadcrumb leading deeper into the corruption that had tainted so many lives. The more Henry examined the figures, the clearer it became that this was no ordinary case of financial misconduct. There were large sums of money moving between shell companies, untraceable transfers to accounts in offshore havens, and most disturbing of all, payments that seemed to coincide with key events in Emily Harper's disappearance.

The deeper Henry delved, the more he realized that Emily's disappearance was just a small part of a larger, more sinister operation. The clinic, which had once seemed like a beacon of hope for the lost and the broken, was revealed as a facade for something much darker. The numbers didn't lie; they painted a picture of exploitation and deceit, orchestrated by powerful individuals who had managed to cover their tracks with disturbing efficiency.

Henry's mind raced as he connected the dots. He recalled his visits to the clinic, the shadowy figures lurking in the hallways, and the hushed whispers among the staff. All the pieces of the puzzle were falling into place. The clinic was a front for a network of corrupt practices that extended far beyond the walls of its dilapidated building. It was a business that thrived on the suffering of its patients, using them as pawns in a game of high-stakes deception.

As he sifted through the records, Henry stumbled upon a name that made his heart skip a beat. The name was tied to several of the transactions, a shadowy benefactor who had provided substantial funding to both Simon's ventures and the clinic. This figure was elusive, with no clear identity and no public record. The name was an enigma, a ghost in the financial system, and Henry's frustration grew as he realized that uncovering this person was crucial to understanding the full scope of the conspiracy.

The files also hinted at a series of meetings and communications between the clinic's management and Simon Harper's associates. It was clear that Emily had been right in her suspicions—Simon's influence extended into every corner of the clinic, ensuring that the facility remained a tool for his manipulation and control. The clinic was not just a place of healing; it was a hub for a network of corruption that exploited the vulnerable.

Henry's thoughts were interrupted by a sudden knock at his door. He glanced at the pile of documents strewn across his table, then hesitated before answering. He had no intention of letting anyone see the evidence he was gathering, not until he had a clearer picture of what he was dealing with.

When he opened the door, he was met by a man in a dark suit, his face obscured by the brim of a fedora. The man's presence was both unsettling and familiar, and Henry felt a shiver run down his spine. Without saying a word, the man handed Henry a small envelope and turned to leave. Henry watched him disappear down the dimly lit hallway before tearing open the envelope.

Inside was a single sheet of paper with a message scrawled in hasty handwriting: "Follow the money. It's not just Simon. Look deeper."

Henry's heart raced as he considered the implications of the note. It was clear that someone else knew about the network he was uncovering, someone who wanted him to dig even further. He had to act quickly. There was no telling who else might be watching or how far the web of corruption extended.

He returned to his desk and continued his analysis, driven by a renewed sense of purpose. The notes suggested that Emily's disappearance was not merely a personal vendetta against Simon, but part of a broader strategy to dismantle the network from within. Emily had become a pawn in a much larger game, and Henry was now deeply entangled in it.

The more he investigated, the more he realized that Emily had been more than just a victim. Her disappearance was a calculated move to expose the corruption, but it was also a desperate bid for freedom from an abusive relationship. The network had silenced her to protect their interests, and Henry had unwittingly become a key player in their scheme.

Henry's frustration grew as he realized the full extent of his own involvement. He had been manipulated by Emily, used as a tool to further her own agenda. The revelation was both infuriating and heartbreaking. He had wanted to save Emily, to be her savior, but instead, he had become a pawn in her game. The weight of his realization was almost too much to bear.

As he continued to analyze the documents, he found evidence suggesting that the shadowy benefactor funding both Simon's ventures and the clinic was a figure with deep connections to the city's elite. This person's influence extended far beyond the financial realm, reaching into the political and social spheres. The network was not just a criminal enterprise; it was a well-oiled machine with the power to manipulate and control those who threatened its stability.

Henry knew that exposing this network would be a monumental task, one that required not only courage but also careful planning. The stakes were high, and the risk of retaliation was significant. But he also knew that he had to see this through to the end. The truth had to be revealed, no matter the cost.

The more he uncovered, the more he felt the walls closing in around him. He was no longer just a disgraced therapist seeking redemption; he was now a key player in a dangerous game of corruption and deceit. The pressure was immense, and the fear of what might happen next was overwhelming.

As Henry pieced together the last of the documents, he began to formulate a plan. He needed to find a way to expose the network without putting himself in immediate danger. He had to be strategic, careful not to draw attention to himself while still pushing forward with his investigation.

He knew that he couldn't do it alone. He needed allies, people who could help him navigate the treacherous waters of corruption and deceit. The network was vast and powerful, and he would need every resource at his disposal to bring it down.

Henry took a deep breath and prepared to contact those who might be able to help him. The road ahead was fraught with danger, but he was determined to see it through. The truth was within his grasp, and he was ready to fight for it, no matter the cost.

As he closed the final folder and looked around at the disarray of his apartment, he felt a sense of resolve. He was no longer just a broken man clinging to the past; he was now a man on a mission, driven by the need to uncover the truth and expose the darkness that had consumed so many lives.

Henry knew that the journey ahead would be fraught with challenges and obstacles, but he was ready to face them head-on. The stakes were high, and the cost of failure was unimaginable, but he was determined to see it through to the end. The truth had to be revealed, and he was prepared to risk everything to make it happen.

With a final glance at the documents spread out before him, Henry stood up and prepared to face the next chapter of his investigation. The road ahead was uncertain, but he was ready to confront the darkness and uncover the truth that had eluded him for so long.

Chapter 8: The Double Life

Dr. Henry Talbot's fingers trembled as he turned the worn pages of Emily Harper's hidden journal. The dim light from his apartment's single, flickering lamp cast long, distorted shadows across the room, creating an eerie ambiance that seemed to underscore the gravity of his discovery. The journal, which he had found buried in a compartment of an old desk at the back of a dusty storage room in the abandoned clinic, was more than just a collection of ink and paper. It was a key—a dark, unsettling key that could unlock the secrets of Emily's disappearance and Henry's own unraveling.

Emily's handwriting was elegant, almost meticulous, reflecting a level of precision and control that belied her outward appearance. Her entries were a blend of personal reflection, strategic planning, and raw emotion, revealing a side of Emily that Henry had never fully grasped during their sessions. As he read through the entries, it became increasingly clear that Emily had orchestrated a complex plan, meticulously designed to escape her oppressive life and frame Simon Harper as the abuser.

The first entry, dated several months before Emily's disappearance, detailed her growing fears and frustrations. She wrote of Simon's increasing control over her life, documenting incidents of emotional and physical abuse with chilling detail. Emily's voice was filled with desperation, yet there was an underlying current of determination that suggested she was not just a victim but a strategic thinker.

"Simon is relentless," she wrote in one entry. "Every day feels like a prison, and he holds the keys. But I have to remain strong. My plan is in motion. Everything will fall into place soon."

The entries that followed were more revealing. Emily had meticulously planned her disappearance, detailing how she intended to disappear from Simon's life and frame him as the villain. She had used her knowledge of Simon's abusive behavior to her advantage, documenting her experiences and conversations that would later serve as evidence against him. Her plan was not only to escape but to exact revenge, making Simon the scapegoat for her troubles.

Emily had not acted alone. The journal hinted at secret meetings with an undisclosed ally, someone who had helped her refine and execute her plan. The exact identity of this person remained ambiguous, but the notes suggested that their involvement was crucial to her scheme. Emily wrote of exchanges involving large sums of money and coded messages, indicating that her plan was supported by powerful, hidden forces.

"I have arranged everything," she wrote. "The escape is set. Simon will be left with nothing but the ruins of his reputation. I've planted the seeds. Now it's time to watch them grow."

Henry's heart raced as he continued reading, the weight of each revelation pressing heavily on his chest. Emily's calculated approach was both impressive and terrifying. She had managed to craft a narrative so convincing that it had almost trapped Henry within its web. The more he read, the clearer it became that Emily's intentions were far more complex than he had initially realized.

The journal also contained personal reflections that humanized Emily in a way that Henry had never seen. Despite the ruthless nature of her plan, there were moments of vulnerability and regret. She questioned whether she was making the right choice, wondering if the pain she was causing Simon and the chaos she was unleashing were worth her freedom.

"Sometimes, I wonder if I'm doing the right thing," Emily wrote. "But then I remember the pain Simon has caused me, the years lost to his cruelty. I must be strong, even if it means becoming something I never thought I would be."

As Henry reached the final pages of the journal, he found a detailed account of the day Emily vanished. She described in precise detail how she had staged her disappearance, making it look like she had been abducted by Simon. The plan involved carefully orchestrated lies and planted evidence to ensure that Simon would be the primary suspect. The journal ended with a chilling note, a declaration of victory and an acknowledgment of the sacrifices she had made.

"I am free now," Emily wrote in her final entry. "Simon will suffer the consequences of his actions, and I will live my life on my terms. The world will see him for what he truly is. I've won."

Henry closed the journal, his mind reeling from the implications of what he had just read. Emily had manipulated him from the very beginning, using his vulnerabilities and professional failings to further her own agenda. The revelation was both a crushing blow and a catalyst for a new understanding of his own role in the unfolding drama.

The room seemed to close in on him as he absorbed the full impact of Emily's deception. The journal had not only unveiled

Emily's intricate plan but had also illuminated the extent of her betrayal. Henry had been a pawn in her game, used to facilitate her escape and undermine Simon. The realization was a bitter pill to swallow, and it left Henry grappling with a sense of betrayal and anger.

He sat in the dim light of his apartment, feeling the weight of the journal's contents pressing heavily on his shoulders. The path to this point had been fraught with uncertainty and peril, but now he had a clear understanding of the role he had played in Emily's scheme. The truth was both liberating and devastating, offering clarity but also leaving him to confront the consequences of his involvement.

As he contemplated his next move, Henry realized that he had to confront the reality of his situation. Emily had planned her escape with a precision that left no room for error, and now he had to face the aftermath of her actions. The journal had given him the answers he had been seeking, but it had also opened a new set of questions about his own role and the price of uncovering the truth.

The revelation of Emily's plan was a turning point in Henry's journey, marking the moment when he fully grasped the extent of her manipulation. It was a sobering realization that forced him to reevaluate his own motivations and the path he had taken in his quest for answers. The journal had provided the final piece of the puzzle, but it had also left him with a profound sense of disillusionment and loss.

In the quiet of his apartment, Henry was left to grapple with the full implications of what he had uncovered. The truth about Emily's plan had reshaped his understanding of the events that had transpired, but it had also cast a shadow over his own actions and decisions. The road ahead was uncertain, and the consequences of his choices would have far-reaching effects on both his own life and the lives of those around him.

Henry's hands trembled as he held the small, leather-bound journal. The dim light from his solitary desk lamp cast long shadows across the pages, making the delicate script seem to dance in the gloom of his apartment. He had discovered this journal hidden in the hollowed-out section of a secondhand book, one that Emily had once mentioned in passing during their sessions. Its presence was a cruel twist of fate, offering him a window into her mind, but also revealing the depth of his own naivety.

The journal was Emily's private chronicle, filled with entries that spanned her time at the clinic and beyond. Henry flipped through the pages, his heart pounding with each word he read. What he found within those pages was both illuminating and deeply disturbing. Emily had meticulously planned her own disappearance, carefully crafting a narrative that would portray Simon as an abuser and rescue herself from a life she had come to despise.

The first entry he read was dated a week before Emily's disappearance. It detailed her growing frustrations with Simon and her plans to frame him. Her writing was coldly calculated, revealing a side of her that Henry had never seen—a side that was both manipulative and ruthless.

October 12, 2022

I'm growing tired of the facade. Simon's charming exterior hides a man who is nothing but a tyrant. Everyone sees the successful businessman, the benevolent husband, but I've seen the real Simon—the man who controls every aspect of my life, stripping me of my dignity and freedom. My therapy sessions are becoming a game now. I need to use Henry to my advantage, make him believe that Simon is the monster he pretends not to be.

I've been planting seeds of doubt in Henry's mind, subtly influencing him to see Simon in the worst light possible. I need him to think that Simon is dangerous, to drive him to expose Simon's true nature. If everything goes according to plan, Henry will be the one to bring Simon's secrets to light, while I walk away from this mess unscathed.

I can't help but feel a twinge of guilt. Henry's own life is falling apart, and I'm using him as a pawn in my game. But it's a small price to pay for my freedom. I've come too far to turn back now. The end justifies the means, doesn't it?

Henry's breath came in ragged gasps as he processed the cold logic in Emily's writing. She had used him as a tool in her elaborate scheme to escape her life and destroy Simon, leaving him as a casualty in her wake. Every note, every session he had shared with her was part of a manipulation designed to make him an unwitting accomplice in her plan.

As Henry continued reading, he uncovered a chilling entry about her final preparations. Emily had arranged for her disappearance to be perfectly timed with Henry's downfall, ensuring that Simon would be under scrutiny just as Henry's career was destroyed. The journal was a testament to her cunning and her complete disregard for the consequences of her actions on others.

November 1, 2022

Everything is almost in place. Henry's obsession with uncovering Simon's true nature is exactly what I anticipated.

I've carefully crafted every detail of my disappearance to coincide with the moment when Henry's own credibility will be questioned. By the time the world realizes what's happened, Simon will be the prime suspect, and Henry will be left to grapple with the mess I've made.

It's almost poetic, really. Simon, who has controlled me for so long, will be brought down by the very person who was meant to help me escape. And Henry, who sought to save me, will be destroyed by the very scheme he unwittingly helped me enact. My freedom is just around the corner, and I can't wait to be free of this life. I just hope that Henry's fall from grace is as spectacular as I've envisioned.

The final entries were a bitter culmination of Emily's plan. Henry felt a surge of anger and betrayal, mingled with a deep sense of regret. Emily's manipulations had not only shattered his career but had also exploited his vulnerabilities. She had twisted his professional and personal life into a grotesque reflection of her own ambitions.

Henry slammed the journal shut, his hands shaking uncontrollably. He sank into his chair, staring at the flickering shadows cast by the lamp. His reflection in the dusty window was a pale ghost of the man he once was, consumed by the revelation of Emily's betrayal.

What hurt the most was the realization that Emily had played him from the very beginning. She had capitalized on his professional pride, his desire to help her, and his own crumbling sanity. In her quest to escape Simon and dismantle her own life, she had destroyed his in the process.

The apartment seemed colder, more oppressive, as Henry grappled with the enormity of the deception. His thoughts swirled in a chaotic dance of anger and disbelief. How could he have been so blind? How could he have been such a pawn in her game?

He reached for the bottle of whiskey on the table, pouring himself a generous measure. The alcohol burned his throat, a temporary balm for the ache that gnawed at his soul. He needed clarity, he told himself, even as the numbness began to settle in. The realization of Emily's betrayal was too much to bear, and he sought solace in the familiar escape of his addiction.

As the night wore on, Henry's thoughts became a tangled mess of fragmented memories and bitter realizations. He replayed the moments he had shared with Emily, scrutinizing every interaction for signs of her deceit. The pain of understanding that he had been manipulated and used was almost unbearable. He had trusted her, believed in her story, and in doing so, had lost everything he had once held dear.

His mind drifted back to the moments when he had felt closest to her—when he believed he was making a real difference in her life. Those memories now seemed tainted, warped by the knowledge of her true intentions. Every kind word she had spoken, every tear she had shed, was now a calculated part of her plan to use him.

The realization also brought with it a gnawing question: what was he supposed to do with this knowledge now? Emily had meticulously orchestrated her disappearance and manipulated the situation to her advantage. Exposing her betrayal could potentially unravel the whole web of deceit, but it would also mean confronting the painful truth of his own complicity.

The journal lay on the table, a silent testament to Emily's duplicity. Henry's mind raced as he weighed his options. He could reveal the truth about Emily's manipulations and the extent of her deceit, but doing so would not only shatter her carefully crafted facade but also leave him vulnerable to the fallout of his own mistakes. The damage to his career and reputation had already been done; unearthing this new layer of betrayal could only serve to deepen the public's disdain for him.

In his heart, Henry knew that the path forward was fraught with peril. He had to decide whether to confront the truth and face the consequences or to protect the remnants of his shattered sanity and let Emily's deception remain buried. The weight of the decision was almost too great to bear.

As dawn approached, Henry's thoughts remained clouded by the fog of his addiction and the gravity of Emily's betrayal. The journal had opened a door to a world of manipulation and deceit that he had never fully understood. Now, he faced the harsh reality of his own role in the tragedy that had unfolded.

With a heavy heart and a mind weighed down by the truth, Henry resolved to confront the situation head-on. He needed to come to terms with the reality of Emily's manipulation and its impact on his own life. The path ahead was uncertain, but he knew that he could no longer hide from the consequences of his actions and the truth of Emily's deception.

Chapter 9: Unreliable Memories

Henry stumbled through the haze of his apartment, the darkness of the room amplifying the disorientation brought on by another restless night. The familiar sting of regret, mingled with the faint smell of stale alcohol, clung to him as he struggled to piece together the fragments of his shattered existence. The shattered remnants of his life, strewn carelessly across the floor, seemed to echo his internal chaos.

The anonymous note had rekindled an obsession that had once consumed him, only now it was deeper, darker, and more perilous. His desperate search for Emily Harper had led him down a path fraught with deceit, corruption, and treachery, but the true weight of his discoveries had only begun to surface. His understanding of reality was wavering, distorted by the drug-fueled fog that clouded his mind. He was unable to discern whether his own memories were genuine or if they had been tainted by his addiction.

As Henry sank into his worn-out armchair, he reached for the crumpled notebook he had found among Emily's possessions. His trembling hands leafed through the pages, each entry revealing a disturbing glimpse into Emily's psyche. The journal had been a pivotal find, shedding light on the carefully orchestrated deception Emily had created. The depth of her manipulation was a harsh reminder of the personal betrayal he had experienced, and it made him question everything he thought he knew about her.

Flipping through the pages, he arrived at an entry dated just days before Emily's disappearance. Her handwriting was hurried, frantic, and tinged with a sense of urgency. It was a stark contrast to the calm, controlled demeanor she had maintained during their sessions. The words leaped off the page, painting a picture of someone who had meticulously planned her vanishing act, leaving no room for error.

I have to be precise. Every detail must be flawless. If Simon suspects anything, he will ruin everything. I can't let that happen. Henry has been my unwitting pawn in this game. He never saw it coming. I'll use his own weakness against him.

The realization hit Henry like a punch to the gut. Emily had not merely vanished to escape her abusive marriage; she had engineered an elaborate scheme to frame Simon while using him, Henry, as a pawn. The enormity of her betrayal was suffocating, and the sense of being used as a tool in someone else's twisted game gnawed at him. He had been manipulated, his career dismantled, and his life left in ruins, all to serve Emily's own agenda.

His mind raced, struggling to reconcile the Emily he had known—the vulnerable, desperate woman seeking help—with the manipulative mastermind revealed in the journal. The lines between reality and delusion blurred further as he attempted to piece together the puzzle of her plan. Had he ever truly understood her, or had he been a mere instrument in her grand design?

Desperation clawed at him as he attempted to make sense of his fragmented memories. He recalled their therapy sessions, their intimate conversations, and the deep connections he had believed they shared. But now, those memories seemed tainted, twisted by the realization that Emily had been playing him from the start.

As the days wore on, Henry found himself spiraling deeper into a pit of self-doubt and paranoia. His addiction intensified, driving him to the brink of madness. The drugs provided a temporary escape from the crushing reality, but they also exacerbated his confusion, making it increasingly difficult to separate fact from fiction. He questioned every interaction with Emily, wondering if her tears and pleas for help had been nothing more than an act.

One evening, as Henry lay in his dingy apartment, his mind fractured by the constant buzz of amphetamines, he was jolted awake by a vivid hallucination. In the midst of the swirling shadows, he saw Emily standing before him, her eyes cold and calculating. Her voice echoed in his ears, a chilling reminder of the betrayal he had endured.

"Did you really think you knew me, Henry?" she taunted, her voice dripping with scorn. "You were just another piece in my game, a means to an end."

Henry's heart raced, his breathing erratic as he grappled with the specter of Emily. The hallucination was a cruel manifestation of his own guilt and confusion, a reflection of the inner turmoil that had become his constant companion. He reached out to touch her, but she vanished into the darkness, leaving him alone with his shattered psyche.

Desperate for clarity, Henry decided to revisit the clinic where Emily had sought treatment. The clinic's decrepit state mirrored the state of his own mind—a place where shadows loomed large, and the truth was obscured by layers of deception. He hoped that by delving into the past, he might uncover something that could shed light on Emily's true intentions.

Arriving at the clinic, Henry was greeted by the familiar sense of foreboding that had accompanied his previous visits. The building, once a beacon of hope for troubled souls, now stood as a decaying monument to corruption. The air was heavy with the scent of mildew and neglect, and the once-bustling corridors were eerily silent.

Henry made his way to the clinic's former director, a man whose involvement in the scandal had been well-documented. The director, now a recluse hiding from the fallout of his own actions, was rumored to have knowledge of Emily's manipulations. Henry hoped that by confronting him, he might uncover further details about the extent of Emily's deception.

The director's office was a cluttered mess, filled with old files and neglected paperwork. The dim light from a single lamp cast long shadows across the room, adding to the oppressive atmosphere. The director, a gaunt man with hollow eyes, looked up from his desk as Henry entered. His expression was a mix of fear and resignation.

"Dr. Talbot," the director greeted, his voice tinged with a hint of familiarity. "What brings you here?"

Henry wasted no time with pleasantries. "I need to know everything about Emily Harper. I know she was involved in something much larger than what I initially thought."

The director's face grew pallid, and he shifted uncomfortably in his chair. "Emily Harper... she was a complex case. We had our suspicions about her intentions, but she was always one step ahead. Her departure was... unusual."

Henry's frustration boiled over. "Unusual? She was manipulating everyone, including me! You must know more."

The director's gaze fell to the floor, his shoulders slumped as if the weight of his knowledge was too much to bear. "Emily was a master of deception. Her manipulations went far beyond anything we could have imagined. She had her own agenda, and she used everyone around her to achieve it."

Henry's heart raced as he listened. "Tell me everything. I need to understand why she did this."

The director hesitated before speaking. "Emily had been plotting her escape for a long time. She used her time here to gather information, to manipulate those who were supposed to help her. Her ultimate goal was to frame Simon Harper, to make him appear as the villain in a story she had written."

Henry's mind reeled. The director's revelation only confirmed what the journal had hinted at, but it was still a jarring confirmation. "So, she used me to destroy Simon's reputation. But why? Why involve me in this?"

The director's eyes met Henry's, filled with a mixture of pity and sorrow. "You were a convenient pawn in her game. Your fall from grace provided the perfect cover for her plans. She knew that if she could destabilize you, it would deflect suspicion from her own actions. It was a carefully orchestrated scheme, and you were an unwitting participant."

The weight of the director's words settled heavily on Henry. The realization of his own insignificance in Emily's grand design was a bitter pill to swallow. He had been nothing more than a tool, a means to an end in her quest for vengeance and escape.

As Henry left the clinic, his mind was a tempest of conflicting emotions. He was overwhelmed by the gravity of Emily's betrayal and the realization that his quest for the truth had led him to a painful confrontation with his own demons. The drugs that had once offered solace now felt like chains, binding him to a cycle of self-destruction and despair.

Henry's return to his apartment was marked by a sense of resignation. The walls seemed to close in on him, the darkness pressing down with a suffocating weight. He was consumed by the knowledge that his quest for justice had only revealed a more disturbing truth—a truth that left him questioning the very fabric of his reality.

In the stillness of the night, Henry's mind raced with the fragments of his recent discoveries. The hallucinations and distorted memories had become his only companions, blurring the lines between past and present. The shadow of Emily's manipulation loomed large, a constant reminder of the treachery that had consumed his life.

As he sat alone in the dim light of his apartment, Henry was confronted with the harsh reality of his situation. His addiction had not only clouded his judgment but had also played a role in the manipulation he had endured. The blurred lines between his own memories and the truth were a testament to the destructive power of his addiction, and the realization was both a source of anguish and a catalyst for his self-loathing.

The journal's revelations had shattered the last remnants of Henry's faith in his own perceptions. He was left grappling with the haunting question of whether he had ever truly known Emily, or if he had been nothing more than a pawn in a twisted game. The betrayal was a bitter pill to swallow, and the quest for truth had led him to a painful confrontation with his own demons.

In the silence of his apartment, Henry's thoughts were a cacophony of regret and despair. The once-promising therapist was now a broken man, consumed by the darkness of his own making. The search for Emily had revealed a deeper truth—one that had cost him everything he held dear.

As the night wore on, Henry was left alone with his thoughts, his mind a tumultuous sea of conflicting emotions. The quest for truth had exposed a deeper betrayal, and the weight of his own failings pressed heavily upon him. In the shadows of his apartment, he was confronted with the harsh reality of his situation—a reality that left him questioning whether the pursuit of truth had been worth the cost.

In the end, Henry Talbot's journey was a tragic reminder of the destructive power of obsession and the fragile nature of truth. The search for Emily Harper had led him to the brink of madness, and the revelations of her manipulation had left him shattered and disillusioned. The once-promising therapist was now a man adrift, consumed by the darkness of his own making, and the price of his quest for truth was a bitter and haunting reminder of the cost of uncovering the truth.

The rain beat incessantly against the grimy windows of Henry Talbot's apartment, the sound merging with the muffled cacophony of sirens and distant shouts from the city below. Henry's surroundings seemed to blur, much like his thoughts, as he sank further into his chair. The room, dimly lit by a single flickering bulb, offered no comfort, only a harsh reminder of his unraveling reality.

Henry's addiction had taken a heavy toll on him. The pills he swallowed with whiskey did little to dull the increasing confusion that clouded his mind. The hallucinations had become more frequent, and the once-familiar boundaries between reality and delusion were now indistinguishable. Each moment seemed to stretch into an eternity, suffused with a sense of dread and disorientation.

He stared at the empty bottle of whiskey on the floor, its label smeared and faded. The glass that had once offered a semblance of solace now seemed to mock him with its emptiness. He felt a profound emptiness within himself, a void that no amount of alcohol or drugs could ever fill. His search for Emily Harper had become a cruel joke, a futile quest driven by delusions and distorted memories.

The images of Emily that danced in his mind were fragmented, surreal. He could see her eyes, wide with fear, but they flickered like shadows on a wall, never quite solidifying into a clear image. Her voice, once soothing, now sounded like a distant echo, lost in the corridors of his deteriorating sanity. Every recollection of their therapy sessions felt tainted, altered by the haze of his addiction.

In an effort to piece together the truth, Henry revisited the files he had managed to salvage from the clinic. He spread them out across the cluttered floor, each page a potential key to understanding the enigma of Emily's disappearance. But the more he read, the more disjointed and unreliable the information seemed. His notes, once clear and methodical, now appeared like the ramblings of a madman.

One file, in particular, caught his attention. It was a collection of Emily's therapy notes, scribbled with his own annotations. As he skimmed through the pages, he struggled to remember the context of each session. The lines between his professional assessment and personal bias had become dangerously blurred. What had once been an objective evaluation now seemed tainted by his own emotions and desires.

His mind wandered back to his last session with Emily, a session shrouded in ambiguity. He recalled her pleading eyes, her desperate attempts to articulate the fear she felt in her marriage. Had he truly understood her suffering, or had he simply been projecting his own sense of inadequacy onto her? The uncertainty gnawed at him, a relentless torment that compounded his confusion.

In a desperate bid to regain some semblance of clarity, Henry decided to revisit the clinic's former director, Dr. Samuel Finch. The man had been a mentor of sorts, someone Henry had respected and trusted before the scandal. If anyone could shed light on Emily's behavior and his own failings, it was Finch.

Henry arrived at Finch's office, now a dimly lit, disheveled space reminiscent of his own apartment. Finch's office had seen better days, the furniture worn and the walls lined with peeling wallpaper. Dr. Finch himself, an elderly man with a tired face, looked up from his desk as Henry entered. His eyes were filled with a mixture of curiosity and concern.

"Henry," Finch greeted, his voice steady but tinged with the weight of the years. "What brings you here?"

"I need answers, Samuel," Henry said, his voice cracking under the strain. "I've been digging into Emily's case, and everything's just... falling apart. My memories, the files—I can't trust any of it anymore."

Finch's gaze softened, though he remained guarded. "Emily Harper was a complex case, Henry. Her behavior was manipulative, but she also had genuine issues. We all knew that. It's no surprise that your recollections might be affected by your current state."

Henry clenched his fists, his knuckles white. "Manipulative? That's what everyone keeps saying. But was it really that simple? Did I miss something crucial?"

Dr. Finch sighed, leaning back in his chair. "Emily had a history of exploiting her therapists' weaknesses. She was a master at using her vulnerability as a weapon. But it wasn't just manipulation for manipulation's sake. There were deeper issues at play."

"Deeper issues?" Henry asked, his voice tinged with frustration. "What do you mean?"

Finch looked thoughtful, his eyes distant. "Emily's background was troubled. She came from a family with a history of abuse, and her relationship with Simon Harper was fraught with control and violence. Her manipulation of her therapists was a defense mechanism, a way to maintain control in a world where she felt utterly powerless."

Henry's mind reeled from Finch's words. He had been so focused on uncovering the truth about Emily's disappearance that he had ignored the broader context of her life. Her manipulation, while painful, was a symptom of deeper psychological scars. The realization left him feeling both guilty and disoriented.

"You're saying I was just another pawn in her game?" Henry's voice was barely a whisper.

"Not necessarily a pawn," Finch said, his tone measured. "You were part of a larger narrative, Henry. Emily used her charm and vulnerability to manipulate those around her, but that doesn't mean she didn't have genuine pain. She wanted to escape her reality, and she used every tool at her disposal to achieve that."

Henry's mind raced as he processed Finch's revelations. The lines between victim and perpetrator, between truth and deception, had become increasingly blurred. He felt like a man trapped in a hall of mirrors, where every reflection distorted reality further.

The visit to Finch had not provided the clarity Henry sought. Instead, it had deepened his confusion, highlighting the complexities of Emily's case and his own role in it. He returned to his apartment, his thoughts a chaotic swirl of doubt and guilt.

As the night wore on, Henry's addiction took hold with renewed intensity. He popped pills with reckless abandon, chasing the fleeting respite they offered. His hallucinations grew more vivid and disturbing, blending with the fractured memories of Emily. He saw her face in every shadow, heard her voice in every creak of the building. The boundaries between his delusions and reality became increasingly indistinguishable.

Henry's mind was a battleground, torn between the desperate need for answers and the crushing weight of his own failings. He had sought the truth, only to find himself entangled in a web of deceit and manipulation that left him questioning his sanity.

As dawn approached, Henry lay in his bed, staring blankly at the ceiling. The room was dark, illuminated only by the faint glow of the streetlights filtering through the blinds. He felt utterly alone, abandoned by both his past and his present. The search for Emily Harper had led him down a path of self-destruction, and the final revelations had left him with a hollow sense of defeat.

In the cold light of morning, Henry knew he faced an uncertain future. His obsession with Emily had cost him dearly, and the truth he had uncovered came at a staggering price. He was left to grapple with the aftermath of his quest, facing the painful reality that the pursuit of truth had irrevocably altered his life.

The rain continued to fall outside, a relentless reminder of the bleakness that enveloped Henry's world. The quest for Emily Harper had left him fractured and lost, and the truth he had sought was now a haunting presence that shadowed his every step. The descent into madness was complete, and Henry Talbot was left to confront the ultimate question: Was the truth worth the price?

Chapter 10: Trapped

Henry Talbot's apartment had become a maze of empty bottles and crumpled papers, an outward manifestation of his shattered mind. The oppressive gloom of his once-pristine therapy office was now mirrored in the squalor of his current living space. The relentless pursuit of truth had devolved into a harrowing descent into paranoia and self-doubt. His investigation had led him to a point where every shadow seemed to harbor a threat, every passerby a potential adversary.

The anonymous messages and his increasingly erratic behavior had drawn the attention of those he'd hoped to avoid. The clinic had begun to notice his probing. Henry had become a marked man, though not yet fully aware of how closely he was being watched.

It was early morning when Henry received a cryptic text message that read, "You're getting too close. Stop digging or face the consequences." The text was from an unknown number, but the threat was clear. The implications sent a shiver down his spine. Who else but the powerful forces he was up against would know about his recent movements?

Desperate for answers, Henry's next step was to confront the former clinic director, Dr. Carl Green, whose mysterious warnings had always lingered in the back of his mind. Dr. Green was an enigmatic figure, rumored to have had a hand in the darker dealings of the clinic, and Henry hoped that a face-to-face meeting might shed some light on the elusive connections he had been struggling to piece together.

The meeting was set for a drab, rundown diner on the outskirts of the city, a place where the light was dim and the atmosphere thick with the scent of old coffee and grease. Dr. Green, now a shadow of his former self, greeted Henry with a nod. His face was gaunt, his eyes hollow, but there was a certain resigned resolve in his demeanor.

"Dr. Green," Henry began, taking a seat across from the older man. "I need answers. You warned me about digging too deep. I need to know why."

Dr. Green sighed heavily, stirring his coffee absentmindedly. "Henry, sometimes it's better not to know what's beneath the surface. The clinic was a cesspool of corruption. You're digging into something that should have stayed buried."

Henry leaned forward, his voice dropping to a whisper. "I'm close to finding out who's behind all this. I need to know what you know about Emily Harper's disappearance."

Dr. Green's face hardened. "Emily Harper was a part of a much bigger game than you realize. She knew things she shouldn't have, and she wasn't the only one. There are powerful people who don't want their secrets exposed. You're not just dealing with a corrupt clinic; you're entangled in something far more dangerous."

Henry's frustration was palpable. "I'm aware of the danger. But if Emily was used as a pawn in this game, I need to understand her role and why she vanished. I need to clear my name and make things right."

Dr. Green's eyes darted around the diner, ensuring that no one was eavesdropping. "Emily was a manipulator. She used people for her own ends, and she had a way of getting what she wanted by exploiting others. Her disappearance was planned, but she wasn't just escaping Simon Harper. She was also setting up a larger scheme."

Henry was taken aback. "A scheme? What do you mean?"

Dr. Green hesitated, then leaned closer. "Emily had a plan to expose the corruption at the clinic and frame Simon Harper. She wanted to dismantle her husband's empire, and in doing so, she decided to use you as a pawn. She knew about your fall from grace and thought that you could be manipulated into furthering her agenda."

Henry's mind reeled. "So, she used me?"

Dr. Green nodded. "Yes. Emily was clever. She manipulated her way into getting your trust and then used your investigation as a smokescreen. She knew that you would become obsessed and that your downfall would be the perfect cover for her escape and eventual revenge."

Henry's hands clenched into fists. "And what about the clinic? What role did they play in all of this?"

"The clinic was a front," Dr. Green said quietly. "It was part of a network that included influential people in the mental health and rehabilitation industries. They used the clinic to cover their tracks and keep patients like Emily under control. Emily's disappearance was meant to serve as a distraction, a way to shift the focus from the real corruption at play."

Henry absorbed this revelation with a mix of anger and despair. "So, if Emily was using me and manipulating the situation, what happens now?"

Dr. Green's gaze was sympathetic. "You're in a precarious position. The people behind all of this are watching you closely. If you push too hard, you risk endangering yourself and those around you. You have to decide how much more you want to dig into this. Sometimes the truth comes with a heavy price."

Henry was lost in thought. The reality of his situation was sinking in. The once-clear path to redemption now seemed obscured by layers of deception and danger. His mind was spinning with thoughts of how to navigate the treacherous landscape ahead.

Dr. Green continued, "There's one more thing you should know. The clinic has been trying to cover its tracks for years. If you're not careful, you might find yourself as part of the collateral damage."

Henry stood up abruptly. "Thank you for the information. I need to think about my next move."

Dr. Green watched him leave, a look of concern etched on his face. As Henry walked out of the diner, the weight of his decisions bore down on him. He had ventured into the heart of darkness, only to find that he was deeper in the labyrinth than he had ever imagined.

The threat that had been hanging over him now felt more tangible. He could sense the danger closing in, and the knowledge that Emily had used him as a pawn left him feeling betrayed and furious. Henry's sense of justice had been hijacked by his personal vendetta, and now he was trapped in a web of lies and corruption.

The city outside seemed to pulse with an ominous energy. Every passerby, every fleeting glance felt like a potential threat. Henry knew that he had to tread carefully. His pursuit of the truth had put him on a collision course with powerful forces, and the consequences of continuing down this path were becoming increasingly apparent.

As Henry made his way back to his apartment, he began to formulate a plan. He needed to stay one step ahead of those who wanted to silence him. His investigation had revealed that Emily's plan was far more intricate than he had realized, and her manipulations had been more calculated and ruthless than he had ever imagined.

Henry knew that the next steps would be perilous. He had to gather more evidence, confront those behind the conspiracy, and ultimately decide how to play his hand. The stakes were high, and the line between right and wrong was increasingly blurred.

In the solitude of his apartment, Henry started to piece together the fragments of his investigation. His addiction was still a constant presence, but the urgency of his situation forced him to focus. He reviewed the notes, documents, and evidence he had gathered, trying to find a way to expose the truth without falling further into the trap set for him.

The path ahead was fraught with danger, and Henry knew that the next phase of his investigation would be crucial. He had to navigate the treacherous waters of deceit, manipulation, and corruption while trying to salvage whatever was left of his life. The search for truth was leading him deeper into a labyrinth, and Henry had to find a way out before it consumed him completely.

Henry's world seemed to shrink with every passing hour. The walls of his dingy apartment, once a sanctuary of solitude, now felt like a prison. The faint whispers of his conscience, drowned by the relentless roar of his addictions, were all but lost. The constant buzz of paranoia that plagued him was only amplified by the disorienting haze of amphetamines and alcohol.

It had been a few days since his confrontation with Simon Harper. Simon's seemingly genuine remorse and denials had left Henry more conflicted than ever. Simon had painted Emily as a manipulative liar, a portrayal Henry had struggled to reconcile with the image he had of her. Each layer of deception peeled back only seemed to expose new, more disturbing truths. As he sank deeper into his investigation, he found himself at the center of a web that grew more intricate and dangerous.

Henry was jolted from his thoughts by the sharp knock on his door. It was a sound he had barely noticed for weeks, lost in his own spiral of self-destruction. He fumbled with the door lock, the tremor in his hands betraying his anxiety. When he finally opened the door, he found himself face-to-face with a young woman he barely recognized. Her nervous eyes and ragged clothes spoke of desperation.

"Dr. Talbot?" Her voice was tinged with uncertainty.

"Yes," Henry replied, squinting through the dim light. "Who are you?"

"My name is Lisa Green. I used to work at the clinic," she said, her voice wavering. "I... I have something that might help you."

Henry's pulse quickened. After weeks of dead ends and fruitless leads, this was a glimmer of hope. "Come in."

Lisa entered hesitantly, taking in the state of Henry's apartment with a mixture of pity and apprehension. She took a seat at the cluttered table, her gaze fixed on a worn folder she clutched tightly in her hands.

"I'm not sure where to start," she said, her eyes darting around the room. "I've been following your investigation. I know what happened to Emily Harper. I know what you've been through."

Henry's curiosity was piqued. "How do you know about Emily?"

Lisa sighed deeply, her eyes welling up with tears. "I was one of the few people who actually knew her well. She was... troubled, but she wasn't the monster Simon made her out to be. I think she was trying to escape something much worse."

Henry leaned forward, his heart racing. "What do you know? What did she want to escape?"

Lisa looked around the room again, her discomfort palpable. "I can't stay long. If anyone finds out I'm talking to you... I could be in danger."

Henry's frustration flared. "We don't have time for games. Just tell me what you know."

Lisa took a deep breath. "Emily was deeply involved in uncovering the corruption at the clinic. She found out things she shouldn't have known. She was trying to expose Simon and his connections, but she was scared. She knew too much, and that made her a target."

Henry's mind raced. "Why would she go missing then? If she was trying to expose them, why wouldn't she just go public?"

Lisa shook her head. "Emily was smart. She knew that going public would only put her in more danger. She had a plan, but things went wrong. She disappeared right after she tried to gather more evidence."

Henry's thoughts were a jumbled mess. "So, what's in the folder?"

Lisa finally opened the folder, revealing a stack of documents and photographs. She slid a few pages toward Henry. "These are copies of emails and financial records that link Simon to the clinic's shady dealings. Emily collected them before she vanished."

Henry's hands trembled as he looked through the documents. The evidence was damning—accounts of illicit transactions, hidden accounts, and suspicious connections. His eyes fell on a photograph of Emily with a man he didn't recognize. "Who is this?"

"That's Julian Meyers," Lisa said. "He was one of the clinic's biggest donors and had significant influence over its operations. Emily was meeting with him just before she disappeared."

Henry absorbed the information, trying to piece together the puzzle. "So, what happened to Emily after she gathered this evidence?"

Lisa hesitated. "She was planning to meet with a journalist to leak the information. But she never showed up. After that, everything went dark."

Henry's frustration bubbled over. "And you're just now coming forward with this?"

"I was scared," Lisa said, her voice cracking. "I saw what happened to others who tried to expose the truth. I knew they would come after me too if I didn't stay silent."

Henry's mind raced with possibilities. The pieces were falling into place, but the picture was still incomplete. "I need to know more. How do I find Julian Meyers?"

Lisa's face paled. "I don't know. He's elusive, and he doesn't show up in public much. But I've heard he has a private office in a high-security building downtown."

Henry felt a surge of hope. "I need to get to him. If he's involved, he might have answers."

Lisa stood up, her expression one of resigned fear. "Be careful, Dr. Talbot. They'll come for you too if they find out you're digging into this."

Henry nodded, already feeling the weight of the investigation pressing down on him. As Lisa left, he stared at the documents spread out before him. The evidence was a breakthrough, but it was also a perilous step into dangerous territory.

With renewed determination, Henry gathered the documents and headed out of his apartment. He had a lead to follow and a man to confront. His path was clear, but the danger was looming ever larger.

As Henry made his way to the high-security building, he could feel the weight of the conspiracy pressing down on him. Every shadow seemed to harbor a threat, every passing face a potential enemy. His mind was a turbulent sea of paranoia and resolve.

The building loomed before him, its sleek exterior reflecting the gray sky. Henry approached the entrance, his heart pounding with anticipation and fear. He had no idea what he would find, but he knew he had to confront Julian Meyers if he was going to uncover the truth about Emily and the corruption that had engulfed his life.

As he stepped into the building, Henry was met with a sleek, modern lobby. The receptionist looked up with a practiced smile, but her eyes betrayed a flicker of curiosity as Henry approached.

"I'm here to see Mr. Julian Meyers," Henry said, trying to keep his voice steady.

The receptionist's smile faltered slightly. "Do you have an appointment?"

Henry hesitated. "No, but it's urgent. I have important information for him."

The receptionist's eyes narrowed, and she reached for the phone. Henry's nerves were on edge as he waited, the seconds stretching into an eternity. He could feel the walls closing in, the danger of his situation becoming more tangible with every passing moment.

The receptionist finally hung up and looked at Henry with a steely expression. "Mr. Meyers is unavailable at the moment. However, I can take your contact information and have him get back to you."

Henry felt a surge of frustration. "I need to speak with him now. It's about the clinic and—"

Before he could finish, the receptionist's phone rang. She answered with a polite but firm tone, her eyes flicking toward Henry.

"Mr. Meyers will see you," she said finally. "Please follow me."

Henry's heart skipped a beat as he followed her to the elevators. The journey up to the higher floors felt interminable, each floor a reminder of the escalating stakes of his investigation. When the elevator doors finally opened, the receptionist led him down a long corridor to a large office door.

She knocked and then opened the door, gesturing for Henry to enter. "Mr. Meyers will see you now."

Henry stepped into the office, his breath catching in his throat. The room was expansive, with floor-to-ceiling windows offering a breathtaking view of the city below. Behind a large mahogany desk sat Julian Meyers, a man in his late fifties with a calm, composed demeanor.

"Dr. Talbot," Meyers said, his voice smooth and measured. "What brings you here today?"

Henry took a deep breath, trying to steady himself. "I have evidence regarding the corruption at the clinic and your involvement. I need to know what you know about Emily Harper."

Meyers' expression remained inscrutable. "Emily Harper? I'm afraid I'm not familiar with the details. What evidence are you referring to?"

Henry laid the documents on the desk, his eyes locked on Meyers'. "This evidence implicates you and Simon Harper in a network of exploitation and corruption. I need answers."

Meyers' eyes flicked over the documents, his face betraying no emotion. "These are serious accusations, Dr. Talbot. What makes you believe these documents are genuine?"

Henry's frustration boiled over. "I have every reason to believe them. Emily Harper was trying to expose this network before she disappeared."

Meyers leaned back in his chair, studying Henry with a penetrating gaze. "Emily Harper was a troubled individual. Her disappearance is tragic, but it doesn't necessarily implicate anyone but herself."

Henry's resolve hardened. "You know more than you're letting on. I need the truth."

Meyers' expression shifted subtly, his calm demeanor masking an undercurrent of irritation. "Dr. Talbot, you must understand that accusations without proof are meaningless. I suggest you be careful with how you pursue this matter."

The tension in the room was palpable. Henry knew he was treading on dangerous ground, but he couldn't back down now. He had come too far to let fear stop him.

"I need to know where Emily is," Henry said firmly. "If you have any information, you owe it to her—and to me—to share it."

Meyers' gaze remained cold and unreadable. "I have no further information to provide. If you have evidence, you should take it to the authorities."

Henry's mind raced, weighing his options. Meyers' refusal to cooperate was expected, but it left him at a crossroads. He had the evidence, but he needed more to make a definitive case. As he left Meyers' office, he felt a renewed sense of urgency. The final pieces of the puzzle were within reach, but the danger was escalating.

As Henry exited the building, the weight of his investigation pressed down on him. He knew that every step he took brought him closer to the truth, but also closer to the edge of his own sanity. The final lead was in his grasp, but the path forward was fraught with peril.

Chapter 11: The Choice

Henry Talbot sat in the small, dimly lit room of his apartment, the only light coming from the flickering candle on his table. The room was cluttered with empty liquor bottles, discarded medication bottles, and crumpled papers. The weight of his investigation had taken its toll on him; his hands trembled slightly as he sifted through the stack of documents laid out before him. The remnants of Emily Harper's case—the pieces of her life that had become his obsession—were now spread out like a jigsaw puzzle he had been desperately trying to solve.

The anonymous note that had reignited his obsession two years after Emily's disappearance now seemed like a cruel joke. The more he uncovered, the more convoluted the truth became. The evidence he had pieced together pointed towards a sinister conspiracy within the mental health and rehabilitation industries. But despite everything, the central mystery—Emily's ultimate fate—remained elusive.

Henry's thoughts were interrupted by a knock on the door. He moved slowly, his body protesting every motion, and peered through the peephole. It was Simon Harper, Emily's estranged husband, standing in the hallway with an unreadable expression on his face. Henry's heart raced, but he knew this confrontation was inevitable. Simon was part of the larger web of deceit Henry was trying to untangle.

When Henry opened the door, Simon's gaze was cold and calculating. "Dr. Talbot," he said, his tone icy. "I hear you've been digging into things that don't concern you."

Henry stepped aside, allowing Simon to enter. "You know why I'm here," Henry said as Simon entered the apartment. "I need to know what happened to Emily. I have evidence that suggests something far more sinister than you're admitting."

Simon's eyes narrowed, but he remained calm. "I've told you before, Henry. Emily was unstable. She manipulated everyone around her, including you. I have no idea where she is now, and frankly, I don't care."

Henry could feel the anger boiling inside him. "You think you can just dismiss this like it's nothing? Emily's disappearance was never just about her. It's tied to a bigger problem, one that involves your financial ties to the clinic and the exploitation of vulnerable patients."

Simon's face hardened. "You're grasping at straws, Henry. I've moved on from that part of my life. Maybe you should, too. You're only making things worse for yourself."

Henry's vision blurred with frustration. "I'm not going to stop until I have the truth. You owe it to Emily, and you owe it to me."

Simon sighed and took a step closer, his voice lowering. "You really want to know what happened? Fine. Emily's been gone for a long time. She staged her own disappearance to frame me and make it look like I was the abuser. She used your professional vulnerability to her advantage, and she succeeded. But you need to let it go, Henry. It's over."

The words hit Henry like a punch to the gut. The idea that Emily had manipulated him so thoroughly—using his own shortcomings and obsession against him—was almost too much to bear. He had spent years trying to uncover the truth, only to realize that he had been a pawn in a larger game.

"I refuse to believe that Emily was just a pawn in her own game," Henry said, his voice shaking. "There's more to this, and I know it. I have evidence that could expose everything—the corruption, the exploitation, and your role in it."

Simon's expression turned smug. "You think you're going to bring everything crashing down with a few scattered documents? You're in over your head, Henry. I've made sure that any incriminating evidence has been buried. You're fighting a losing battle."

Henry's mind raced. He had come so far, but now he faced a stark choice: continue digging and risk everything, including his own fragile sobriety, or let it go and accept the consequences of his past actions. His obsession had consumed him, and he could feel the weight of his decisions pressing down on him.

"Leave now," Simon said, turning to leave. "I don't want to see you again."

Henry watched as Simon walked out of his apartment, the door closing with a finality that echoed in the empty room. He felt a surge of desperation and anger. If Simon was right, if Emily had used him as a pawn, then what was he really fighting for? The truth had become a distorted and painful reality, and Henry was left grappling with the ramifications of his own choices.

As he stared at the pile of evidence on his table, Henry felt a profound sense of betrayal. Emily had manipulated not just Simon, but him as well. The lines between right and wrong, truth and deception, had become increasingly blurred. He was left with the haunting realization that his own actions might have contributed to the chaos.

Henry sank into a chair, his mind spinning. He could almost hear Emily's voice in his head, taunting him with the knowledge that he had been used to further her own agenda. The sense of betrayal was overwhelming, and he felt a deep, gnawing emptiness.

The apartment was silent except for the ticking of a clock on the wall, a reminder of the time slipping away. Henry's hands trembled as he reached for the bottle of whiskey on the floor. He needed something to dull the pain, to escape from the crushing weight of his reality. But even as he poured himself a drink, he knew that it wouldn't solve his problems. The choices he had made, the paths he had taken, had led him to this point.

As the amber liquid burned its way down his throat, Henry struggled to focus. The evidence he had uncovered was damning, but it was also incomplete. There were pieces of the puzzle missing, and he needed to find them before he could fully understand what had happened.

He glanced at the stack of documents on the table—notes, financial records, and personal journals. They were all fragments of a larger story, a story that had been twisted by deceit and manipulation. Henry had to decide whether to continue his search for the truth or to accept the possibility that he had been part of a larger conspiracy all along.

The decision weighed heavily on him. If he exposed everything he had uncovered, he risked not only his own reputation but also the lives of innocent people who had been caught in the crossfire. If he chose to remain silent, he would be complicit in a cover-up that could allow the corruption to continue unchecked.

Henry's mind raced through the possibilities. He knew that exposing the truth could lead to a reckoning, but it could also destroy the lives of those who were already suffering. His own redemption was at stake, but so was the potential for justice.

The confrontation with Simon had left Henry reeling, and the burden of his choices was almost too much to bear. He needed to make a decision, and he needed to make it soon. The final pieces of the puzzle were within reach, but the consequences of uncovering the truth were more daunting than ever.

As the night wore on, Henry found himself at a crossroads. The choices he made would determine not only his own future but also the fate of those who had been affected by the web of deceit that had ensnared them all. The road ahead was fraught with danger, and Henry was left to grapple with the ultimate question: Was the truth worth the cost?

Henry Talbot stood alone in the cluttered, dimly lit apartment, the room suffused with the faint, acrid odor of whiskey and stale cigarettes. The chaos of his life seemed to have seeped into the very walls of this place, rendering it a shrine to his downfall. He glanced around, taking in the scattering of old therapy notes, bottles of pills, and empty liquor bottles that littered the floor. It was in this ruin of his former life that he faced the most significant decision of his career, and perhaps of his existence.

The evidence he had gathered over the past weeks lay before him, a damning collection of documents and records that could both clear his name and expose the horrifying corruption of the clinic and its associated network. He had everything necessary to unravel the tangled web that had ensnared Emily, Simon Harper, and the corrupt figures lurking behind the scenes. It was a choice that could redeem him or plunge him further into the abyss.

The phone call had come just hours ago. Simon Harper's voice on the other end had been a cold, calculated whisper. The message was clear: Henry could stay silent and preserve what little stability he had left, or he could expose the truth and risk everything, including his own fragile grip on sobriety.

As Henry sat at the makeshift desk in his apartment, his mind raced through the implications of Simon's ultimatum. The pile of evidence was a heavy burden, both literally and metaphorically. On one hand, it was the key to revealing the darkness within the mental health and rehabilitation industries. On the other, it was a weapon that could cause immense collateral damage, affecting innocent lives who had been unwittingly caught in the crossfire.

He stared at the photographs and documents strewn across the desk, images of Emily's last days, financial transactions, and records linking Simon to the clinic's illicit activities. His hands trembled as he picked up a photograph of Emily, taken during a brief moment of vulnerability that he had managed to capture in a rare moment of clarity. Her face was a mixture of fear and defiance, a stark reminder of what was at stake.

Henry had spent weeks piecing together Emily's elaborate scheme. He knew now that her disappearance had been a meticulously crafted ruse, designed not only to escape her abusive marriage but to frame Simon and create a scandal that would dismantle his life. Emily had used Henry as a pawn, manipulating his own vulnerabilities and flaws to serve her agenda.

But now, Simon's threat loomed over him. The choice was more than just a matter of professional redemption; it was a personal battle between maintaining his fragile sobriety and the risk of losing everything he had left. Simon had hinted at dangerous consequences should Henry decide to go public. The stakes were no longer confined to his career but extended to his very existence.

Henry could almost hear Simon's voice echoing through his mind, a haunting reminder of the threat that lingered. Simon had promised that staying silent would allow Henry to keep his life as it was—a shattered semblance of normalcy. But exposing the truth, Simon had warned, could lead to dire consequences. The fear of losing everything was palpable, a constant undercurrent that gnawed at his resolve.

He took a deep breath, trying to steady the pounding in his chest. The decision was not just about the evidence; it was about whether he could face the reality of what Emily had done and the impact his actions would have on others. The truth was a double-edged sword, capable of both redemption and devastation.

In the dim light of the apartment, Henry found himself revisiting the memories of his sessions with Emily. The sessions had been filled with a mixture of empathy and confusion, his own personal struggles often clouding his professional judgment. He had seen glimpses of Emily's pain, her fear of Simon, and her desperate need for escape. But he had also been a willing participant in her manipulations, drawn into a dangerous game of deceit.

He picked up a worn notebook filled with Emily's scrawled handwriting, a glimpse into her psyche and the planning that had gone into her disappearance. The entries detailed her feelings of entrapment, her desire to escape, and the steps she had taken to execute her plan. But they also revealed a calculated mind, one that had used Henry's professional ethics against him, exploiting his weaknesses to further her own goals.

As he read through the entries, a sense of betrayal washed over him. Emily had not only manipulated him but had used his own failures to fuel her escape. The knowledge was both crushing and clarifying. It was a painful reminder of how deeply he had been ensnared in her scheme.

The phone rang again, breaking the oppressive silence. Henry glanced at the caller ID and saw Simon's number flashing on the screen. It was as if Simon knew the exact moment to strike, to add more weight to Henry's already strained decision.

With a resigned sigh, Henry answered the call. Simon's voice was smooth and menacing, a reminder of the power and control he wielded.

"Henry," Simon said, his tone dripping with a false sense of cordiality. "I trust you're considering your options carefully. I wouldn't want you to make a decision you'll regret."

Henry's grip on the phone tightened. "What exactly do you want from me, Simon? What's the price of silence?"

Simon's laughter on the other end was chilling. "The price is simple: your compliance. Stay silent, and you can continue your life without further disruption. Expose the truth, and you may find yourself in a very precarious situation."

The threat was clear, but so was the moral dilemma Henry faced. He had the power to bring the corrupt network to light, to hold those responsible accountable. But doing so would require him to make a choice that could unravel the lives of many, including those who were innocent but caught in the crossfire of his revelations.

Henry's thoughts drifted to the people he had met along the way—those who had been part of the support group, those who had suffered in silence. They had all been victims of a system that had exploited their vulnerabilities, and now, he had the chance to fight back.

But what about his own redemption? Could he truly be forgiven for his past mistakes, and what price would he pay for seeking it? The lines between right and wrong were increasingly blurred, and Henry was caught in a vortex of his own making.

He took another deep breath, trying to clear his mind. The decision was not just about exposing the truth; it was about confronting his own demons and determining whether he could live with the consequences of his actions.

As the minutes ticked by, Henry weighed the possibilities. He could expose the truth, risking Simon's threat and the potential fallout. Alternatively, he could remain silent, preserving his precarious stability but leaving the corrupt system intact. The choice was a heavy one, with each option carrying its own set of repercussions.

In the end, Henry knew that the decision was not only about him but about the people who had been wronged, the ones who deserved justice. The weight of the evidence, the potential harm, and the ethical considerations all played a role in the choice he had to make.

He glanced once more at the pile of documents and photographs, the pieces of a puzzle that could either mend or shatter his life. The realization hit him hard: the truth, no matter how painful, was a force that demanded to be reckoned with.

With a final, determined breath, Henry set his jaw. The path ahead was fraught with danger and uncertainty, but he knew that the time had come to make a choice. The price of truth was steep, but the cost of silence was equally high.

As he made his decision, Henry felt a strange sense of clarity amidst the chaos. The decision was made, and he would face whatever consequences came with it. The path to redemption was unclear, but it was a path he had to walk.

In the end, the choice was not just about his own fate but about the future of those who had suffered in silence. Henry was ready to confront the consequences of his actions and face whatever came next, knowing that the truth, no matter how dark, was a force that could no longer be ignored.

Chapter 12: The Price of Truth

The morning light seeped through the grimy windows of Henry's apartment, casting a dim glow over the cluttered space. Empty bottles of whiskey and amphetamine vials lay strewn across the floor like shattered dreams, remnants of a life unraveling at the seams. Henry Talbot sat at the edge of his bed, clutching a crumpled piece of paper in his trembling hand. The note was a final piece of the puzzle—a damning piece of evidence that could either clear his name or seal his fate.

For weeks now, Henry had been navigating a labyrinth of deception and betrayal. His pursuit of the truth about Emily Harper had led him to dark corners of corruption, personal revelations, and now, a final confrontation. He had uncovered evidence that could expose the clinic's nefarious dealings and Simon Harper's manipulation, but he knew that doing so would come at a cost.

Henry's mind swam with the memories of Emily—her fear, her desperation, her calculated cruelty. It was as if he were in a fog, trying to piece together a puzzle with missing pieces. The image of Emily, once a beacon of hope, had transformed into a haunting specter of manipulation and betrayal.

With a heavy heart, Henry stood up and made his way to his cluttered desk, where the evidence lay scattered. The documents, photographs, and notes chronicled the corruption within the clinic and Simon's involvement. He had discovered that Emily's disappearance was not a simple case of escape but a meticulously planned scheme. Emily had faked her own death and framed Simon for the abuse she had suffered, all while using Henry as an unwitting pawn in her elaborate game.

As he sifted through the evidence, Henry felt the weight of his decisions pressing down on him. The anonymous note that had reignited his obsession, the secret journal revealing Emily's plan, and the disturbing truths about the clinic all pointed to one undeniable conclusion—Emily was alive and had orchestrated a complex web of deceit.

The phone rang, shattering the silence of the apartment. Henry glanced at the caller ID and saw Simon's name flashing on the screen. His heart raced, and he hesitated before answering.

"Henry," Simon's voice came through, cold and calculated. "I hear you've been busy. I hope you've found what you were looking for."

"I have," Henry replied, his voice strained. "I know the truth, Simon. I have the evidence that proves your involvement in the clinic's corruption and Emily's manipulation."

There was a pause on the other end of the line. Henry could almost hear the wheels turning in Simon's mind. "And what do you plan to do with this information?" Simon asked finally.

Henry took a deep breath, trying to steady his nerves. "I'm going to expose it. The world needs to know what you've done."

Simon's laugh was chilling. "You're making a mistake, Henry. You think you're the hero here, but you're just a pawn. Exposing the truth will destroy lives—innocent lives. Are you prepared for that?"

The question hung in the air, heavy with implication. Henry knew that revealing the truth would have repercussions far beyond his own suffering. The clinic's patients, the staff who were unwittingly involved, and even Emily herself—everyone would be affected.

"I don't have a choice," Henry said, his voice resolute. "I need to make things right."

Simon's tone softened, becoming almost sympathetic. "I understand, Henry. But remember this—if you expose the truth, you'll be dragged down with it. Your name, your reputation, everything you've worked for will be destroyed. You'll lose everything."

The call ended abruptly, leaving Henry alone with his thoughts. He sat in the dim light of his apartment, staring at the evidence before him. The choice he faced was agonizing. On one hand, there was the moral imperative to reveal the corruption and clear his name. On the other hand, there was the harsh reality of the consequences—a world of hurt and destruction that would follow.

Henry's thoughts drifted back to his interactions with Emily—the therapy sessions, the moments of vulnerability, and the final confrontation that had led to her disappearance. He had believed that he was helping her, that he was saving her from a terrible fate. But now, he realized that Emily had used him as a pawn in her own twisted game.

He picked up the journal, flipping through the pages that detailed Emily's plan. The entries were cold and calculating, revealing a woman who was willing to do anything to escape her life with Simon. Her meticulous planning, her manipulation of Henry, and her ultimate betrayal were laid bare before him.

The door to his apartment creaked open, and Henry looked up to see Mia standing in the doorway. Her face was lined with concern, her eyes reflecting the pain of her own struggles. She had been a crucial part of his investigation, providing him with insights into Emily's life and connections.

"Mia," Henry said, his voice filled with exhaustion. "I didn't expect to see you."

"I came to see if you were alright," Mia replied, stepping into the apartment. "I heard about your confrontation with Simon. I'm worried about you."

Henry shook his head, a bitter smile on his lips. "I'm not sure if there's anything 'alright' left. I have the evidence to expose everything, but I'm facing a choice I never expected."

Mia walked over to him, her gaze falling on the scattered documents. "You've uncovered the truth, Henry. You've done more than most people would dare. But you need to think about the impact of your actions."

Henry nodded, feeling the weight of her words. "I know. But I can't ignore what's right. I need to expose the corruption, even if it means losing everything."

Mia placed a comforting hand on his shoulder. "Whatever you decide, just remember that you're not alone. You've helped me, and I want to help you in return."

The words were a small comfort in the storm of Henry's emotions. He knew that Mia's support was genuine, but it did little to ease the crushing reality of his situation. The decision he faced was not just about right and wrong—it was about survival and sacrifice.

Henry stood up, his resolve hardening. "I need to do this, Mia. For myself, for the people who have been hurt, and for the truth. I have to expose what's been hidden, no matter the cost."

As he prepared to make his final move, Henry felt a surge of determination. He was ready to confront the consequences of his actions and face the fallout of revealing the truth. The road ahead was uncertain, but he knew that the price of silence was far greater than the cost of truth.

With the evidence in hand and a heavy heart, Henry Talbot set out on the path that would determine his future. The reckoning was at hand, and he was ready to face it head-on, knowing that the price of truth was a burden he had to bear.

The finality of the truth was overwhelming. As Henry Talbot sat in his dingy apartment, surrounded by the detritus of his ruined life, he felt a hollow victory. The revelations of the past weeks, the endless search, and the unraveling of Emily Harper's elaborate deception had led to a climactic exposure of corruption and betrayal. Yet, as the pieces fell into place, Henry found himself more isolated than ever, confronting the true cost of his pursuit.

The media had gone wild with the news of the scandal. The once-revered therapist had become the center of a storm. The clinic, Simon Harper's deceit, and Emily's manipulative scheme had all been laid bare for the world to see. The headlines screamed about a massive cover-up involving powerful figures, but Henry's name was prominently featured as the tragic figure caught in a web of deceit. The public's perception was mixed; some saw him as a martyr, others as a pawn. For Henry, however, it was the fallout from these revelations that cut the deepest.

He stared at the dimly lit room, the flickering light from a broken lamp casting long shadows against the peeling wallpaper. The apartment, once a symbol of his disgrace, now felt like a tomb—a stark reminder of the life he had lost. His addiction had taken its toll; the once sharp mind now grappled with bouts of confusion, and the pain of his reality was often numbed by the bottle and pills that littered the floor.

Henry had thought that exposing Emily's plot would redeem him, but instead, it had pushed him further into a spiral of despair. His professional license was irrevocably lost, his reputation tarnished beyond repair. Even the small solace of vindication felt hollow, like a mirage in a desert of regret. The investigation had shown that Emily had not just staged her disappearance but had meticulously manipulated Henry to destroy his career as a part of her elaborate revenge against Simon.

His former colleagues, once supportive, now avoided him. Those who had once admired his intellect and empathy now looked upon him with disdain or pity. The news stories had painted him as a tragic figure, a once-great therapist brought low by personal and professional failings. But the public's compassion did little to heal the wounds inside him. The letters of support he received were drowned out by the harsh, unrelenting judgments of his past actions.

In the quiet solitude of his apartment, Henry's only company was the alcohol and the amphetamines that had become his solace. The constant numbness was a temporary escape from the ceaseless torment of his thoughts. He'd hoped that with the exposure of Emily's schemes, he might find some sense of closure, but it only seemed to deepen his torment. The sight of Emily's face in the media, her fabricated victimhood now a symbol of deceit, was a constant reminder of how he had been manipulated.

Henry's mind often drifted back to his last encounter with Emily, the revelations of her hidden journal, and the final confrontation with Simon. It was clear that Emily had orchestrated her disappearance with a cold, calculating precision. Her plan had involved much more than just escaping her abusive marriage; it was a sophisticated scheme to undermine Simon, which had the unintended consequence of ruining Henry's life in the process. Her ability to manipulate him, to use his own vulnerabilities against him, was a testament to her calculated nature.

As Henry continued to drink away his sorrows, his thoughts were interrupted by a knock on the door. He had been expecting this. The relentless pursuit of the truth had made him a target, and now, as he faced the consequences of his actions, the repercussions were beginning to knock on his door.

He opened it to find a young woman standing there, holding a folder tightly to her chest. She introduced herself as a journalist, one of the few who had followed the story closely and had been sympathetic to his plight. She had come to offer him an opportunity to tell his side of the story, to shed light on the personal toll of the scandal and his journey through the wreckage of his life.

Henry, though initially hesitant, agreed. He needed to speak, to lay bare the personal cost of the truth, if only to find some semblance of peace. The interview was set to take place in the modest apartment, the setting for the final chapter of his story. The journalist began with gentle questions, probing into Henry's experiences and the impact of the revelations on his life.

"I suppose you want to know how it feels," Henry began, his voice tinged with the bitterness of his reality. "To know that my life has been turned inside out, that the very person I tried to help turned out to be the architect of my ruin."

The journalist nodded, encouraging him to continue. Henry took a deep breath and recounted his journey—the passion and idealism that had once driven him, the betrayal by Emily, and the subsequent unraveling of his career. He spoke of his addiction, the numbing haze that had become his refuge, and the haunting realization that his quest for truth had cost him everything.

"I thought," he continued, "that exposing Emily's deception would restore my name, that it would somehow redeem me. But what I've found is that truth, when it comes at such a cost, can be a double-edged sword. I lost myself in the process, and now I'm left with the fragments of a life that was once full of promise."

The journalist listened intently, her notepad filled with the raw details of Henry's experience. The interview continued for hours, delving deep into the emotional and psychological toll of his journey. Henry spoke candidly about the personal demons he faced, the fractured relationships, and the struggle to come to terms with his own role in the tragic events.

As the interview concluded, Henry felt an unexpected sense of relief. For the first time in a long while, he had articulated his pain and disillusionment openly. The journalist thanked him and promised to handle his story with the sensitivity it deserved.

With the departure of the journalist, Henry returned to his solitude, the weight of his revelations sinking in. The media's attention had shifted, the public's interest waning. He was left to grapple with the aftermath of his actions and the wreckage of his once-promising life.

Days turned into weeks, and Henry's apartment remained a sanctuary of solitude. His addiction persisted, a constant companion in his quest for escape. Yet, amidst the haze of substance abuse, he began to find moments of clarity. The realization that his pursuit of truth had cost him dearly became a central theme in his reflections.

In the quiet of his apartment, Henry found himself revisiting the final entries in Emily's journal. The pages, filled with her calculated plans and manipulations, were a stark reminder of her ability to exploit others for her own gain. Yet, despite the bitterness and anger, Henry found a trace of empathy. Emily's actions, however twisted, were driven by a desperate need to escape a life of abuse and control.

The juxtaposition of his own suffering with Emily's motives presented a complex moral landscape. Henry's quest for justice had exposed the corruption and deceit but had also illuminated the fragility of human lives entangled in a web of manipulation and revenge. The truth, while painful, had also revealed the underlying vulnerabilities and complexities of those involved.

As Henry continued to navigate his own demons, he began to grapple with a sense of acceptance. The truth had come at a staggering price, but it had also provided insight into the human condition. The cost of revealing the truth was not just professional or personal; it was a profound existential reckoning with the nature of justice, redemption, and the cost of uncovering hidden realities.

In the end, Henry's story was one of tragedy and reflection—a cautionary tale of the price paid for seeking the truth amidst deception and manipulation. As he faced the consequences of his actions and the wreckage of his life, he found solace in the realization that, despite the suffering, there was a measure of understanding in the chaos. The journey through the labyrinth of deceit had left him scarred, but it had also provided a glimpse into the complexities of human motives and the harsh realities of truth.

As the final chapter of his story unfolded, Henry Talbot's legacy was one of profound loss and introspection. His name would be remembered not just for the scandal and the scandalous revelations but for the haunting journey through a world of deception and the personal cost of uncovering hidden truths. The price of truth, as he had come to understand, was a heavy burden—one that demanded a reckoning with the deepest facets of the human soul.

Don't miss out!

Visit the website below and you can sign up to receive emails whenever Michael Ferguson publishes a new book. There's no charge and no obligation.

https://books2read.com/r/B-A-CKNW-TOWZE

BOOKS 2 READ

Connecting independent readers to independent writers.

Did you love *Cold Comfort*? Then you should read *Obsessed With Shadows*[1] by Michael Ferguson!

[2]

In the sleepy town of Crestwood, 17-year-old Jake Marshall is an average high school senior with a passion for true crime podcasts and mystery novels. His quiet life takes a dramatic turn when the body of Lily Thompson, a popular and seemingly perfect classmate, is discovered in the nearby woods. The town is thrown into shock, and the investigation into Lily's death quickly becomes the talk of the community.

Intrigued and driven by his fascination with crime, Jake begins to delve into the case on his own. What starts as a

---

1. https://books2read.com/u/mZWRKl

2. https://books2read.com/u/mZWRKl

mere curiosity soon turns into an all-consuming obsession. As Jake digs deeper, he uncovers a series of unsettling truths about Lily's life that nobody else seems to know. He discovers that Lily was entangled in a complex web of relationships and secrets that reveal her life was far more complicated than her public persona suggested.

Jake's investigation leads him to receive anonymous threats, and he begins to notice that people around him are acting strangely. His friendships start to deteriorate, his academic performance suffers, and his once-stable life begins to unravel. The deeper Jake gets into the case, the more dangerous it becomes, as he realizes that someone is watching him and manipulating events to their advantage.

The investigation brings Jake face-to-face with unexpected allies and potential suspects. He uncovers hidden motives and dark agendas, all while struggling to maintain his own sanity. As he gets closer to the truth, the lines between reality and obsession blur, leading him into a dangerous game where he's not sure who he can trust.

In a shocking climax, Jake learns that the true mastermind behind the murder has been manipulating him all along, setting him up as the perfect scapegoat. He is faced with an impossible choice: to clear his name, he must commit a crime that would make him the very monster he's been hunting. The book concludes with Jake reflecting on the cost of his obsession and whether he can find a way to rebuild his life and seek redemption.

Obsessed with Shadows is a gripping and intense mystery that explores the fine line between passion and obsession, the consequences of pursuing the truth, and the impact of uncovering dark secrets. It takes readers on a thrilling journey through suspense and intrigue, challenging them to consider how far one might go in the quest for answers.